She was his wife in all ways but one

"Don't push me away, Bryce" Claudine pleaded. "The scars from the accident don't matter to me. All I know is that I love you".

Bryce held her rigidly at arm's length. "You don't understand what you're asking of me", he said through clenched teeth. His constricted voice betrayed the conflict raging within him.

Tears coursed down her face as Claudine shook her head in helpless frustration. But Bryce turned away and quickly strode into his bedroom. The click of the key turning in the lock was final.

Other
MYSTIQUE BOOKS
by CAROLINE GAYET

For a free catalogue listing all available Mystique Books,
end your name and address to:

TIQUE BOOKS
uth Priest Drive, Tempe, AZ 85281
649 Ontario St., Stratford, Ontario N5A 6W2

Passionate Stranger

by CAROLINE GAYET

MYSTIQUE BOOKS

TORONTO·LONDON·NEW YORK
HAMBURG·AMSTERDAM·STOCKHOLM

PASSIONATE STRANGER/first published August 1981

ISBN 0-373-50138-2

PRINTED IN CANADA

Chapter 1

"Claudine? Do you know where my blue shirt is?" An impatient male voice came from the bedroom accompanied by sounds of slamming drawers and closet doors.

Claudine didn't look up from the pattern that she was tracing into the material before her. A gleaming curtain of chestnut hair hid her face. "I haven't seen it, Bryce. Did you take it to the laundry?"

The thud of something falling against the wall was immediately followed by her husband's voice, now loud with anger. "Could you at least come here and help me look for it? I'm trying to pack, you know."

Claudine raised her head with a sigh. The familiar argument was starting again. After only eight months of married life she could tell when Bryce was going to start complaining. Her slim body tensed and a look of anxiety crept into her wide brown eyes. She tried to keep her voice patient as she replied. "I'm really busy, Bryce. I've got to get this pattern done.

A lady from London is coming here to Paris tomorrow to see the collection."

Bryce strode into the living room, his dark eyes narrowed and his jaw set in anger and frustration.

"You and your silly little boutique. You always have to put it first before everything!"

"I don't put it first! It's just that there are certain responsibilities with running a business...."

Bryce's derisive laugh stopped her and she could feel the last reserves of her patience ebbing away.

"I don't know why you waste so much of your time in such ridiculous ways." The scorn in his voice became more pronounced. "You would do better to spend your time at home like a good wife."

Claudine's fair skin flushed with rising anger. "I happen to enjoy what I do. And my shop is as important to me as your job is to you."

"Important? A stupid little dress shop where foolish women come in and chatter over the latest fashions! You call that important?"

"It is to me! It's what I do and I don't think you have to be so snide about it."

"And I suppose that our marriage isn't so important to you? Perhaps you think it's a waste of your precious time to take care of our home?"

"I do take care of it! I certainly do a lot more around here than you do!" Claudine raised her voice as Bryce left the room. "I don't see what's so terrible about having to find your own shirt for a change."

"I can't wait until we move to Autun," Bryce shouted. "Maybe then you'll settle down and try a little harder to be a proper wife."

Claudine felt tears of anger and frustration fill her eyes. Bryce refused to understand how much her boutique meant to her, and he didn't seem to see how much it hurt her when he derided all that she was trying to do.

She put down the pattern she was working on and got up to help Bryce pack, feeling angry with herself for letting him make her feel guilty for doing something that she knew was right.

Bryce looked up as she came into the bedroom. "Oh, don't bother, Claudine. I did this well enough before I got married, I guess I can do it just as well now."

His voice was filled with such disgust that Claudine felt stunned, as if he had slapped her across the face. She felt a sob constrict her throat as she ran into the bathroom and slammed and locked the door.

She buried her face in her hands and wept. How had they come to this after only eight months of being married? She loved Bryce, but he was so self-centered and demanding. Try as she would, they just couldn't seem to get along with each other. There were just too many differences between them and he made no attempt to be understanding.

After a brief interval there was a knock at the door.

"Claudine?" Bryce's voice was still tense. "I'm sorry. Come out."

Claudine didn't reply and made no move.

"Come on, Claudine, I have to leave now."

Choked with the pent-up sobs of days and months of frustration, Claudine still didn't reply. A moment later she heard the apartment door slam shut behind Bryce.

HALF AN HOUR LATER, completely exhausted, Claudine finally emerged from the bathroom. Wearily she filled the kettle for coffee. When it was brewed, she took her cup back into the living room and settled into her own particular chair. *Why have things gone so wrong*, she asked herself miserably.

She thought back to when she had first met Bryce. It had been more than a year since she'd come to Paris from the United States. Her design business was doing better than expected, so she had decided to take a short vacation in Portugal. Bryce was staying at the same hotel and he had been so handsome and attentive that she'd immediately fallen in love with him. They had spent all their time in each other's company, and once back in Paris, they had continued seeing each other regularly. And then, after having only known each other for two months, he had asked her to marry him and she had readily accepted.

Claudine could vividly recall the night that Bryce had proposed to her. They had just been to the theater and they had decided to walk the short distance back to her apartment, enjoying being alone together in the crisp fall evening. A sudden rainstorm forced them to take shelter in a nearby café. They had sat together listening to the sound of the falling rain outside and drinking café au lait in the cheerful warmth.

Bryce had reached over and taken her hand in his. For a long moment he had gazed into her eyes. Then he had murmured in a low, emotional voice, "Claudine, this is the way I always want it to be. Please say you'll marry me."

She had smiled ecstatically at him through sparkling tears. "Oh, yes, Bryce."

The wedding ceremony had been quiet and simple. Bryce had invited a few friends but no relatives. His parents were dead and his older half brother and half sister, whom he never saw, were out of the country.

Claudine's mother and father flew over to Paris from Chicago. They were proud of their daughter's success with her boutique and impressed by Bryce's responsible job and obvious devotion to Claudine.

At first married life seemed an extension of their happy courtship, but day by day little disagreements appeared like clouds on a clear horizon. Bryce had apparently been spoiled for many years by an indulgent mother, and he didn't take kindly to sharing Claudine's attention with her boutique. She couldn't make him understand what it meant to her, and he refused to share any aspects of his own work with her.

Gradually, their earlier pleasure in each other was eroded by the realities of their daily lives. Claudine felt helpless. The breach between her and Bryce kept growing and she wasn't sure how it all had started or how she could stop it from getting bigger or even close the gap.

She had put so much work into getting the shop started and it was all just beginning to pay off. It was true that they didn't really need the money, but the boutique was more than that to her. It was what she enjoyed doing; it was her career.

The company he worked for, Gevaudan Chemical Research Company, had recently decided to build new laboratories in Autun, a city southeast of Paris, and Bryce had been chosen to head the project there. They were going to have to move and Bryce wanted Claudine to give up her boutique. That subject had caused even more bitter disagreements between them.

Claudine sighed deeply as she rose to get ready for work. She had succeeded in business through determination and hard work, so she certainly wouldn't give up her marriage without a struggle. Her small chin set resolutely.

Claudine was sorry that she had let Bryce leave in such a state. She knew from experience that these business trips took about a week and that if Bryce was angry when he left he was usually in a worse mood when he returned. She vowed that she would try harder to be understanding when he got home.

FIVE DAYS AFTER BRYCE HAD LEFT Claudine received a telephone call.

"Mrs. Chevalier?" asked the cold and official-sounding voice on the other end of the line.

"Yes?"

"It's your husband. . . . I'm afraid there's been a terrible accident."

Chapter 2

Claudine's thick chestnut hair tumbled over her shoulders as she huddled in a corner of the taxi and looked out the window at the darkened countryside passing by. Everything looked so peaceful, so quiet, as if forever unaffected by the tragedies of the people who lived and loved and died on its soil.

While her dark eyes gazed at the calm scene outside, Claudine's mind was in a turmoil. Again and again she went over the few facts that she had been given, trying to understand them, desperately attempting to glean from them some indication of where these sudden events were leading her.

The policeman who had called from Bourg-Saint-Pierre hadn't been very helpful. All that he had been able to tell her was that on the fifteenth of August, Bryce had been driving along a secondary road leading to the mountains. His car had left the road, plunged fifty feet into a ravine and caught fire. Bryce, though badly burned, had been able to pull himself out of the wreck and had been taken to the Mountain Spring Clinic near Bourg-Saint-Pierre.

The police hadn't been able to get in touch with her sooner because all of Bryce's papers had been destroyed in the fire and they had had to conduct a long series of investigations in order to establish his identity. They had no idea what Bryce had been doing on that back road nor could they tell her how the accident had occurred, except to suggest that perhaps he had been drinking, something Claudine knew that Bryce never did while driving.

When she called the clinic a Dr. Leroux, who had operated on Bryce, insisted on talking to her. He had tried his best to be kind and reassuring but the news was very bad. Bryce had been in a coma since the accident and his condition was extremely critical. The doctor did not feel that he could make any definite prognosis and suggested that Claudine come to the Mountain Spring Clinic as soon as she could.

For a moment Claudine had panicked. Her only close friend, Sophie, was out of town, and when she tried to contact Bryce's closest friend, William Sancenay, he was out and couldn't be located. A feeling of immense helplessness overwhelmed her. She had never had to face such a crisis alone. Her fear and panic nearly paralyzed her and for a moment she didn't know what to do or where to turn. But the panic had been subdued by the urgent need to act, to do something. So she had called the airport and made reservations for the flight to Chambéry and had quickly packed her suitcase.

That had been a mere six hours ago and as Claudine stared out the window of the taxi on her way to the clinic, she had no way of determining what was going to happen next. As yet, she could not make sense out of what had happened.

The hospital came into sight about nine miles outside of Bourg-Saint-Pierre. It was built of white stone and nestled into the hillside, overlooking a valley surrounded by mountains. Its large balconies facing south, along with its seclusion, gave it the appearance of some sort of resort.

Dr. Leroux was waiting for Claudine when she arrived. He was a man of about forty, small, dark, with twinkling gray eyes and a mustache. He tried to sound optimistic as he explained to her the nature of the hospital.

"We're quite fully equipped to handle such emergencies, Mrs. Chevalier. Mountain Spring was originally designed as a sanatorium for tuberculosis patients, but the success of modern treatments of the disease has all but eliminated the need for such hospitals, and the owners decided to convert the property into a surgical clinic specializing in the treatment of accident victims."

The doctor went on to explain all of the equipment that the hospital possessed for such emergencies. But something in his attempt to be reassuring rang false to Claudine.

"Doctor, could you please get to the point and tell me what my husband's condition is?"

"The truth is," he replied slowly, "your husband is extraordinarily lucky to have survived. He has suffered multiple fractures. But even more serious, he has suffered severe burns over much of his body. In such burn cases there is always the great possibility of complicating infections."

"What exactly are his chances of surviving?"

"It's a very difficult case, Mrs. Chevalier. I'd say his chances are less than fifty-fifty."

Claudine had thought that she had prepared herself for the worst, but when she heard the doctor's negative prognosis, it was almost more than she could bear. Her small shoulders slumped and she had to clamp her full lower lip between her teeth to keep it from trembling. She looked down at her small hands, which were clenched tightly together, and fought back the tears that threatened to overflow at any moment.

"May I go in and see him?" she finally managed to ask in a small voice.

"I'm afraid we can't allow that at this time. We've had to isolate him in a sterile room in order to reduce the chances of infection. I'd like to assure you that we're accustomed to dealing with emergency cases and with plastic surgery. It will be necessary for us to make both cosmetic and physical repairs to your husband. However, Professor Montaubert, the director of the clinic, enjoys an international reputation in this field. At the moment he is spending three months in China, but I hope the confidence he has vested in me will help to assuage your worries. I promise you that we'll do everything in our power to save your husband."

Claudine made no reply, and possibly interpreting this as a sign of doubt, the doctor continued. "Your husband can't be moved, but if you'd like the opinion of another specialist, Paris isn't far away and you could perhaps call someone to come here."

If the accident had happened closer to Paris Claudine would have considered having Bryce taken care of in one of the city's hospitals. But she didn't know of any specialist who could be reached in the middle of August when everyone was on vacation. "I don't know anyone," she replied to the doctor. "Our own doctor is away for the month."

"Yes, it's certainly hard on people who get sick in the summer. It's fortunate that the fools who found your husband brought him here."

Claudine stared at the doctor in surprise. "Fools?"

"Weren't you told? They drove him here them-selves in their own car. We've told people time and time again never to move an accident victim, that to do so could easily kill him. But the people who found your husband, who must have been lying uncon-scious for several hours, lifted him up and brought him here in their own car. They could very easily have killed him, but in fact they probably saved his life. We immediately put him into the intensive care unit. As I said, your husband was lucky."

"And the people who brought him here?"

"We were rather rude to them, I'm afraid, and I think they understood that we were very angry with them for breaking such a basic rule of first aid. They left without giving their names."

"I would have liked to thank them," Claudine said simply.

A strange look passed across the doctor's face. "Perhaps thanks should wait until later. But I don't want to sound too pessimistic. Your husband is young and seems to be fairly strong, and he may recover quite well, but...."

At that moment a willowy blond nurse entered the doctor's office; he gestured toward her. "Oh, Mrs. Chevalier, I'd like you to meet Jeannette. Jeannette is the nurse who is looking after your husband. She's very intelligent and I can assure you she's extremely qualified for this kind of work."

Jeannette had a kind and sympathetic smile. "I'm afraid it's forbidden to go into his room," she said, "but you may see your husband through the observation window. Providing the doctor has no objection."

"None at all," said Leroux. "But please don't expect to see much."

The sterile room was separated from a small anteroom by a glass wall through which the patient could be seen at all times. The walls of the room were shiny enamel. There was a cast-iron bed at one end and on it a body enveloped in a kind of shell, the head covered with bandages, like a mummy, with plastic tubes connecting it to lifegiving fluids.

It was hard for Claudine to imagine that this motionless mound of sterile bandages was her husband. It was almost too painful for her to think of the Bryce she had known lying in there burned and broken and helpless.

The nurse turned toward her. "Try not to be disheartened. We have his condition stabilized. I've been assisting Dr. Leroux for five years and have seen him work miracles. He has the hands of a magician and is probably superior to Professor Montaubert, despite the fact that he isn't as well-known."

Jeannette led her over to a desk and helped her fill out some necessary papers.

"Have you notified his family?"

"His parents are dead," Claudine replied.

"Has he any brothers or sisters?"

"There's a sister who lives in Canada, and a brother somewhere. But he hasn't heard from him for twelve years."

"Did they disagree?"

"Not really. These two are his father's children by his first wife, and they didn't accept his second marriage very well. The daughter got married when she was eighteen and the boy left France when he was sixteen. My husband hasn't heard from either of them since."

The nurse's questions made Claudine realize, for the first time, how isolated she and Bryce were. Her own family was all back in the United States. The only time they had even met Bryce was at the wedding.

"Have you found a place to stay?" Jeannette asked, breaking into Claudine's train of thought.

"No. I haven't even stopped to think about it. I don't know this area at all." Claudine began to feel more and more helpless.

"There's a little hotel in Villars-les-Saint-Pierre, the closest village. Would you like me to call and get a room for you?"

Jeannette's sympathetic and helpful manner was comforting, and Claudine thankfully allowed her to make all the arrangements.

"The clinic car will take you to Villars-les-Saint-Pierre," the nurse told her as she led her to the exit. "Try to rest. If there's any change in his condition I'll call you. I hope the hotel doesn't seem too uncomfortable. You may be there for some time."

THE HOTEL WAS A PLEASANT PLACE, built mainly for accommodating skiers in the winter. Claudine's room looked out onto the promenade, which was lined with linden trees.

Claudine sat down on the bed, too emotionally

drained even to unpack her small suitcase. Things
made hardly any more sense than they had that
morning. Why, why did all of this have to happen?
Bryce was usually such a good driver, he'd never
been in a car accident before. And what was he doing
on that small back road in the first place?

Claudine remembered the bitter argument she and
Bryce had had just before he left and guilt assailed
her. If only she had been more patient and loving,
none of this would have happened. She had let him
leave angry, giving him no chance to apologize. She
put her head in her hands and, surrendering to the
weight of remorse and grief, was shaken by a torrent
of weeping. And sobbing, she fell asleep.

CLAUDINE PASSED THE NEXT FEW DAYS in a sort of confused daze, either at the Mountain Spring Clinic or at
the hotel. And all that she did at either place was
wait.

Every day she would stare through the observation
window at the unchanging, shapeless mass of
bandages that was Bryce, waiting for some kind of
indication of improvement, thinking of all the ways
she could have made their lives better, all the kind
words she could have said but never did. And every
day the oppression of her guilt grew.

Often, in the hallways and corridors of the
hospital, Claudine would meet other patients. Some
were in plaster casts, others had crutches, others had
stitches on their faces. But what Claudine noticed
most about them were the curious looks, almost of
repulsion, that they seemed to give her. It was as if
the possibility that Bryce might live made them
afraid. Even Jeannette, when assuring Claudine that

she thought Bryce would live, had a curious, pitying tone in her voice. Claudine couldn't understand why, if her husband was going to live, the nurse would feel sorry for her.

The day after Claudine arrived at Mountain Spring she was visited by one of Bryce's colleagues who had come to see if there was anything she needed. On behalf of his company, he offered her a surprisingly large loan, which she accepted. On leaving, he held her hand for a minute, his gaze warmly sympathetic. But his manner, too, was pitying.

By the end of the week, Bryce's condition was giving them more cause for hope. He was still on the critical list, but his heart was strong and he seemed to be responding to treatment.

Finally, one morning when Claudine arrived at the hospital, Dr. Leroux was waiting with good news.

"Your husband has regained consciousness."

A great feeling of relief washed over Claudine. "Is he out of danger?"

"No, the danger's far from over. But it's a very good sign."

"Does he know I'm here?" Claudine asked hesitantly.

"Yes, and I promised him he could see you through the window."

The doctor accompanied her to the glass window. Bryce's position hadn't changed. He still lay motionless beneath the bandages, but now there was a pair of dark glasses shading his eyes. Claudine wondered what he was thinking. Was he remembering the argument they had had just before he left? Perhaps he was even wishing that she wasn't there.

Claudine blew him a kiss, hoping that somehow he would understand how sorry she was.

Bryce made steady progress, but Dr. Leroux still seemed anxious. And the expression on his face when, three weeks after the accident, he said that unless there were unexpected complications, Bryce was out of danger, seemed to contradict the good news.

Claudine studied the doctor carefully. "Is there something wrong? Is there something you haven't told me?"

Leroux looked at her intently. "There's nothing I haven't told you. But until now I considered it premature to discuss with you the full implications of your husband's injuries."

His tone sparked a sudden fear in Claudine. "What's wrong? Will he be an invalid?"

"No, not at all. I promise to return him to you whole and in good working order. But it's important to explain to you what we have been obliged to do. Your husband suffered burns over most of his body, as you know. In days gone by he would have died of septicemia or dehydration. With transfusions and antibiotics we were able to keep him alive. In certain areas, we've been able to make direct grafts from his own skin. In other areas, where the burns were too extensive, we had to resort to tissue from skin banks and make temporary transplants, which we'll gradually replace with skin from his own body."

"Yes, I know that. What's the point?" Claudine's fear was mounting with the doctor's evident hesitation.

"I have to make it clear to you that we've been forced to replace, piece by piece, much of the skin on his body, and to perform extensive surgery on his limbs, his hands included. The extent of his fractures also obliged us to carry out a number of bone grafts that will change his build, maybe the length of his limbs, and certainly the shape of his hands."

"But he won't be crippled in any way?"

"No. He won't be crippled. It's just...well, the condition of his face was terrible. It wasn't only burned, the bone structure was also severely damaged. We had to rebuild everything, including his nose, his cheekbones, his eyebrows, even his scalp, which was badly torn. What I'm trying to say is that he's not going to look anything like he did before. He's going to be completely different."

What he was trying to say suddenly hit Claudine. Now she understood Jeannette's compassion and the fear she had seen in the other patients' eyes.

Chapter 3

Bryce had been so handsome! He had also been very vain about his good looks. Claudine's mind grew dizzy as she thought about what her husband's reaction would be. It was going to be immensely difficult for him to accept being disfigured. She recalled how once, when the barber had made a mistake in cutting his hair, Bryce had been in a rage for days, bitterly complaining about something so small that no one else would even notice. She shuddered to think of the torture he was going to go through now, and for the rest of his life!

"Perhaps it would have been better if he'd died," Claudine murmured.

"What? Simply because his profile is changed?" Leroux sounded slightly offended. "I give you my word that after the first few months, when you have had time to get used to it, both of you will accept his new looks and voice."

"You've changed his voice, as well?" Claudine was surprised.

"His throat was damaged also, and his vocal cords were torn. But we have been able to repair them."

Claudine had been worried for so long about whether Bryce would live or die that she hadn't even stopped to consider the actual extent of his injuries.

"What about his eyes? Are they going to be alright?"

"His eyes were relatively unhurt, but there was some injury to the eyelids. However, these days it's a fairly straightforward procedure to repair damage of this kind. The results we can obtain through the use of laser beams are incredible. All the repair work will take time, several months perhaps, but I can guarantee the results."

"Months!" Claudine held her head in her hands. "Why did you perform the surgery on his face without finding out what he looked like originally?"

Leroux sighed patiently. "Because of the nature of his injuries I had to work extremely fast. In the case of some facial blemishes we have to operate over a period of years. In your husband's case I would prefer to keep him here and do all the work at one time. At the moment there are too many possible complications for me to be able to tell you exactly how long it will take. Believe me, I did what was best under the circumstances."

The implications of all this information nearly sent Claudine into a state of shock.

"Does Bryce know?"

"Not yet."

"May I be there when you tell him?"

"Please try to be a little less anxious, Mrs. Chevalier. My belief is that since your husband has been so near death, he will attach less importance to his looks than you seem to imagine."

Claudine knew Bryce better than the doctor did. Still, there was something in what he said. She hoped that he was right.

"Is Bryce in any pain?"

"I'm afraid that burns are very painful. We have him on morphine but we can't give him enough to obliterate the pain. It only eases it somewhat."

The next month passed much the same as the first, except that now Claudine's worries shifted from whether or not Bryce would live to how he was going to live with his disfigurement. And this new worry caused her as much pain and guilt as the news of the accident had.

Despite his increasing strength, Bryce still had to be kept isolated in the sterile room. And every day Claudine watched him through the window, although there was nothing new to see.

Jeannette, who assisted Dr. Leroux in changing the bandages, brought Claudine news of his steady progress. "His face is going to be completely normal," the nurse told her, trying to ease some of Claudine's worries. "These days it's nothing to remodel a nose or a chin, or even to rebuild eyelids or lips from strips of membrane taken from inside the patient's cheeks."

Claudine turned away, visibly disturbed.

"I'm sorry," Jeannette apologized. "But to me a successful operation is like an old master is to a painter. In a way, Dr. Leroux's work on your husband is a work of art. The scars on his face are barely visible."

Claudine found it hard to discuss Bryce's injuries, but Jeannette convinced her that the more she understood the operation, the more she would be able to accept it and help Bryce.

"Is the rest of his body very badly scarred?" she asked tentatively.

"There are a lot of marks on his body, I'm afraid. The worst parts are the areas that were burned, his back, arms and legs. There are some scars on his stomach and thighs where the grafts were taken. I doubt if he'll be walking around much in his bathing suit."

"Is his chest that bad?"

"No, his chest was hardly touched. But there are quite a few scars on his back."

And so Bryce's condition improved, slowly but steadily. A couple of times over the next few weeks his close friend, William Sancenay, a free-lance press photographer, came and visited. Claudine had never cared much for William. There always seemed to be something sly and devious about him. But he was Bryce's closest friend, so she did her best to get along with him.

Claudine's prolonged stay in the small town was eased by the kindness and thoughtfulness of the people there. She became quite friendly with a few of them and they were always asking how Bryce was and if there was anything they could do for her.

Claudine knew that she should go back to Paris, at least to take care of the duties and obligations that were mounting up in her absence. Her boutique had remained closed for nearly two months, and if it hadn't been for the loan from Bryce's company, their debts would have been enormous. As it was, they still owed a great deal of money.

But Claudine didn't want to leave. Even though she knew that her presence wasn't doing Bryce any good, it eased her conscience. She still felt an immense amount of pain and guilt; perhaps if she had been a better wife none of this would have happened. She felt that just by staying she proved, at least to herself, that things were going to be different when Bryce got better and could return home.

One day when Claudine arrived at the clinic, Dr. Leroux asked to speak to her in his office.

"When I was changing his bandages this morning, Bryce asked for a mirror. I was forced to explain to him all that we had done."

Claudine felt extremely agitated. "How did he react? Did he seem terribly upset?"

"Well, it was a shock for him to see himself, as could be expected. But he seemed to take it pretty well. Also, he sent this note to you."

Claudine was surprised. "I didn't know that the could write yet," she said, taking the note handed to her.

"He can only use his left hand, and that not very well."

On the piece of paper was a single, awkwardly printed line.

Please don't worry, darling. I love you.

The note upset Claudine. It did not sound at all like Bryce. It had been a long time since he had talked to her about love, and he had never called her "darling." Claudine could only imagine how much pain and suffering he must be going through for such a change to have taken place.

It was just a few days later that Mr. Charreau, the president of Bryce's company, came to visit Claudine. The purpose of his visit was to assure her that the company would cover all the hospital expenses and that Bryce's position would be kept open for him. He told Claudine that the new plant wouldn't be completed before the spring, and by then Bryce would be in a fit condition to return to his beloved research.

"Do you expect Bryce to be posted in the provinces for long?" Claudine asked him.

"I hope so! If our research succeeds we'll have a gold mine at our fingertips. Didn't he tell you about it?"

Claudine shook her head no.

"So much the better. I like discreet colleagues."

Claudine didn't tell Mr. Charreau that the reason Bryce concealed the nature of his work from her was not discretion; it was just that he considered her too stupid to understand it.

The information that they were still going to have to move to Autun, and would be there for a great length of time, helped Claudine make up her mind about what to do with her boutique. She had considered trying to find someone to run it while she was away, since she was so uncertain of the future. But now she was resolved to sell it, which is what Bryce had wanted her to do all along.

This decision greatly buoyed her spirits. It seemed to her that she could finally do something for Bryce, something that would assuage her constant feelings of guilt. She at last found a vent for her overpowering desire to act, to do something. She quickly prepared to return to Paris.

Before she left, Claudine went one last time to see Bryce through the observation window. The bed had been raised and he was half sitting, watching her. He waved his left hand, which was covered with a strip of white gauze that left his fingers free. His fingers looked shorter and squarer than Claudine had remembered. Then he took off his dark glasses.

Through a small slit in the bandages that covered his face, Claudine could see two dark eyes—eyes that looked like a stranger's, observing her curiously.

Claudine was so upset by the sight of them that she went to see Dr. Leroux before she left the clinic. Seeing that she was quite shaken, he asked her what was wrong.

"It's his eyes. Bryce took off his glasses and I didn't recognize his eyes."

Quite unexpectedly the doctor started to laugh.

"That's impossible! His eyes are practically the only part of him that hasn't been changed."

"But they seemed to have a different expression, a different shape."

"Well, his eyebrows and eyelids are different and that might account for some of it. But I promise you, his eyes are the same. As for the difference in expression, I wouldn't judge too much by that. It's pretty hard to recognize him through all those bandages. Try putting on a mask and looking at yourself in the mirror. I'd be surprised if you'd recognize yourself."

Claudine felt a little silly for having reacted so strongly and was about to leave when the doctor stopped her. His level gaze was stern. "You're going to have to be very careful, Mrs. Chevalier. Your husband is going to need a wife who will support him without any reservation. If you attach a great deal of attention to every detail, you'll do him an enormous amount of harm. You would be doing him a favor if you would overlook all the little changes in his appearance."

She took the doctor's advice to heart and promised herself that she would never again react in such a childish manner.

WHEN CLAUDINE ARRIVED IN PARIS that evening it was raining. The exuberant energy that had accompanied her decision to sell the boutique had been worn away by the long, dreary train ride. She was sore and tired and the amount of work that lay before her was beginning to depress her. Everything in the apartment was just where she had left it when she had hurried out weeks ago. The dirty dishes were still in the sink and all the food in the refrigerator was spoiled.

Claudine set her suitcase down and wearily sank into an easy chair. A strange feeling of uneasiness came over her as she looked around the room. Something in the small, neat apartment seemed to be out of place. *It's just from having been away to long*, she reassured herself as she got up to go into the bathroom. She ran hot water over fragrant bath crystals and slowly removed her clothes. When the tub was full she got in, letting the hot, perfumed water ease her tired body. As her aches slowly began to loosen their hold, Claudine tried to get her mind to relax. She had been tense for so long it was only with difficulty that she could get herself to forget her troubles for even one evening.

After the water in the tub had grown cold Claudine got out and dried herself on a rough blue towel. Putting on the fluffy white robe hanging behind the door, she padded out of the bathroom and over toward the bedroom.

She had taken only two steps into the room when she suddenly froze, her eyes riveted to the wall in fear.

One of the first things that Claudine had done when she and Bryce had moved into the small apartment was to hang up the wedding picture of the two of them. Bryce had thought it was sentimental, and perhaps it was, but it was Claudine's favorite picture of them and it had made the apartment seem much homier. She had hung the picture up on the far wall of the bedroom, between the closet and the window. It was at that spot that Claudine now stared as she clutched her robe tightly around her.

The picture was gone.

The fact that someone had been in her apartment caused Claudine to shudder. She looked quickly around the room as if she expected the intruder still to be lurking there. Her hands were shaking as she checked the valuables she had left in the apartment. The camera, her jewelry, everything seemed to be there. Then, with a strange feeling of disbelief, she looked on top of her dresser where she kept two small pictures, one of herself and one of Bryce. The picture of her was still there. But the one of Bryce had been removed from the gilded frame.

Claudine sat down on the edge of the bed, her hands clenched tightly together, trying to gather her whirling thoughts. She felt as if she were in some bizarre nightmare. She forced herself to be calm, telling herself that there had to be a logical explanation.

She remembered that the superintendent had a key to the apartment. Quickly pulling on a pair of jeans and a blouse, she ran downstairs to see if he had let anyone into the apartment while she was away.

The superintendent told her that William Sancenay had been by the week before, and since he had recognized the man as a friend of theirs, he had let him in.

Claudine walked slowly back upstairs, trying to make sense of what was going on. Why would William take down all the pictures of Bryce? She could understand his being worried about how Bryce was going to react to his new appeareance, and it would perhaps be easier for Bryce if he wasn't confronted with pictures that showed how handsome he used to look. But how could William be so presumptuous as to remove the pictures without first asking her about it? Claudine decided that the only way to find out would be to call William.

"Yes," William admitted unabashedly over the phone, "I destroyed the pictures."

"But how could you do that without asking me?" His casual unconcern fueled her indignation.

"Bryce asked me to."

"When could he have?" Claudine demanded.

"When I was at Villars-les-Saint-Pierre. He told his nurse to ask me to destroy all his photos—without exception."

Claudine's anger swelled. It was humiliating that Bryce should have secretly asked this man, whom she disliked and mistrusted, to enter their home and destroy their property.

"I still don't understand why he couldn't have asked me," she declared hotly.

William sighed impatiently. "He asked me because he was afraid that you would want to keep some."

This stopped Claudine for a moment. It was true. Then a sudden thought struck her.

"Just a minute! The doctor hadn't told Bryce yet when you were at Villars."

"Claudine, my dear, do you think he needed to be told? You can feel a broken nose and a smashed jaw."

Claudine knew that what William said made sense. She wondered why she hadn't realized before that as soon as he regained consciousness, Bryce must have been able to guess the extent of his injuries. The fact that he had waited so long before asking for a mirror and that he had obliterated all evidence of the face he had had previously revealed the extent of his anguish.

"Did you destroy *all* of his photos?" she asked in a subdued tone.

"I think so. If I missed any, please destroy them."

Claudine hung up the phone and rifled through every drawer in the apartment. But William had carried out his mission thoroughly. Even the negatives were gone, along with a number of identity cards in Bryce's desk—an expired passport and his military papers among others.

Bryce's orders impressed on her even further the full extent of his distress. For herself, Claudine was sorry that William had been so careful. She would have liked to keep some of the photos, even if they did bring back some unhappy memories.

Tired and more distressed than ever, Claudine finally fell into a restless sleep.

Chapter 4

Claudine was having lunch with her friend Sophie. Sophie, a tall, slim brunette with lively blue eyes, was the only true friend that Claudine had in Paris. Claudine often confided in her, and in fact, Sophie was the only person who knew about the troubles Bryce and Claudine had been having in their marriage.

They met at their favorite café in the Latin Quarter, and over a light lunch of chicken crepes and white wine, Sophie listened sympathetically to Claudine's long story.

"So now what do you plan to do?" Sophie asked when Claudine had finished giving her all the details of the accident and subsequent surgery.

"Bryce's boss assured me that he was going to keep Bryce's job open for him. I guess we'll still be moving to Autun."

"And what about your shop? Are you still planning to find someone to run it for you until you get back?"

"From the way it sounds, I think we'll be in Autun for quite a while. I guess the best thing for me to do is to sell the boutique."

Sophie was astounded. "Sell it! After all the work you put into it? And what will you do in Autun anyway?"

"I know, Sophie. And believe me, it wasn't an easy decision. But I really think it's for the best."

Sophie looked at her intently. "I know it's probably none of my business, but Claudine, dear, you and Bryce were getting along so poorly before all this happened, what makes you think you're going to get on any better now?"

Claudine stared fixedly at her wineglass. "Things are different now, Sophie."

"I expect so! Before he was merely difficult to live with. Now he'll be impossible."

"Don't say that. It was my fault, I never tried hard enough to give him what he needed."

"Claudine! I know you're feeling sorry for Bryce right now, and it is terrible what's happened to him, but try to be realistic. You tried as hard as anyone could reasonably expect. You and Bryce are just two different people with different interests and different goals."

"But he's still my husband, and I still love him."

Sophie reached across the table and pressed Claudine's hand. "Don't misunderstand me. I know you love him. But I think that right at the moment you're reacting more out of guilt and pity. Why don't you just keep the boutique until you can see what's going to happen. You can always sell it later if you want."

Claudine looked steadily into Sophie's eyes. "Maybe a lot of what I'm feeling is guilt, but Bryce

needs me now and I'm going to stick with him as long
as he wants me to. And what better way to show him
that than to sell my boutique?"

Since Claudine's mind was so obviously made up,
Sophie pressed her no further. Instead, Sophie volun-
teered her help in trying to find a buyer. If Claudine
insisted on selling the shop, her friend was determined that she get the best deal possible.

It took three weeks to find a buyer, settle the terms
and take care of the legal paperwork. Every night
Claudine called the hospital in Mountain Spring to
check on Bryce's progress. Jeannette told her every
detail; everything was coming along satisfactorily,
but slower than Claudine had hoped. Bryce was still
in isolation, although every day he was getting
stronger.

The sale of the boutique was finally concluded,
and with Sophie's help Claudine was able to make a
good profit. She was able to pay off most of her debts
and still have a sum of money left over.

Finally Claudine could remain in Paris no longer.
Professor Montaubert was due to return to the clinic
and Dr. Leroux and his team were to leave on holiday. The doctor wanted to see Claudine before he
left, so she packed her bags and made preparations to
leave.

On her last night in Paris, Claudine had trouble
falling asleep. All the anxiety and distress that had
been pushed aside during the hectic activity sur-
rounding the sale of the boutique returned with renewed force. How would Bryce—who had always
been so difficult and hard to please—react to his new
self? Would he become even more bitter and de-

manding? Or would he turn to her and let her give
him the comfort and support he would so drastically
need? Claudine had no way of knowing, but she had
made her choice. She had sold the boutique and she
was going to stick by him for better or for worse.

As she drifted off to sleep, she remembered the
note he had scrawled: "I love you."

Maybe things would be different now.

CLAUDINE ARRIVED at Mountain Spring on the last
Saturday in October, the day before Dr. Leroux was
to leave. Winter was in the air, the mountaintops
were covered with the first snow, and the countryside was gray and still. The hotel was badly heated,
and despite the welcome she received, Claudine
found her surroundings depressing.

At the clinic, Jeannette's mind was entirely on her
holiday.

"I'm going to the Balearic islands," she announced.
"I'm going to get tanned, swim, dance, sleep and
forget about the whole world!"

Claudine looked at her enviously, wishing that she
could go somewhere and forget the whole world,
too.

Jeannette must have seen the look for she added
softly, "I would have liked to be here when you see
your husband without his bandages. You'll be so
pleased."

Dr. Leroux, who was going to the Caribbean, was
equally reassuring.

"If I didn't know your husband was out of danger,
I wouldn't be going," he assured her. "Professor
Montaubert will be taking care of him personally.
I'm sorry I won't be able to see the professor before I

go, but he's been kept in Paris for an extra day and I can't get my reservations put back. Rest assured that I'll leave him a complete case history. We are very used to working together."

"Will you be away long?" she asked, still not happy that he was going.

"A month. And I hope you'll have left by the time I get back. I think the professor will take your husband out of isolation almost immediately. After that we just have to keep an eye on how the scars heal and work on his morale. This is where you will come in. Your husband will have to face some very difficult moments and he is going to need all your help."

"Is his face that bad?"

"Not at all. But one has to learn how to live with a completely new physique, and it's up to you to help him. Pretend to recognize him, and if you are disappointed, try to keep it to yourself. Above all, don't ask to see his face before he's ready to show it to you."

Claudine was surprised. "You mean he'll have the bandages on even when he gets out of isolation?"

"Yes. He may wish to keep the bandages on longer than is strictly necessary. He'll be nervous about your reaction and will probably put off the ordeal as long as possible."

Claudine nodded, although she wondered if the doctor wasn't attaching more importance to her reaction than Bryce would. He certainly hadn't set too much store by her judgment in the past.

"I'll do as much as I can for him, doctor. I hope I'll be able to help, I feel so sorry for him."

"Try not to make him too aware of that. He doesn't need pity."

Claudine saw Bryce that evening through the observation window. He wasn't wearing his dark
glasses and once again she noticed how strange his
eyes seemed. But conscious of the doctor's advice,
she controlled the expression on her own face and
smiled at Bryce.

Upset that the doctor in whom she had placed her
trust and confidence was gone, Claudine was doubly
disappointed when, a few days later, she had her first
meeting with Professor Montaubert.

The professor was cold and aloof, and though he
had more clinical experience than his assistant, he
seemed to lack Leroux's human warmth. Without ap-
pearing to be interested in the case, he gave her his
impression of Bryce's condition. However, the report
he gave was excellent and he launched into a long
eulogy on the results obtained by Dr. Leroux.
"Miraculous," he kept saying, "miraculous." His
mind was obviously elsewhere.

Montaubert also introduced her to his personal
nurse, a new member of the staff whom he had
engaged on his recent stop in Paris. The nurse's name
was Lucy. She was small and plump, with a very firm
manner that was in distinct contrast to her appearance. She seemed pleasant enough, but Claudine
couldn't help missing Jeannette.

THREE DAYS LATER the professor decided that Bryce
had been in isolation for long enough and moved him
to an ordinary room.

Claudine was trembling with apprehension. After
so long she was finally going to be able to sit close to
him, to hold his hand. He'd still be covered with bandages, but just the thought of being that close to him

and talking to him made her knees feel weak as she walked to his room.

Bryce was sitting up in bed, his head bandaged down to the neck, dark glasses covering his eyes. Claudine sat down on the bed next to him, uncertain of how to begin. What words could she use to tell him all that she had been through and that she was willing to give him everything she could.

"Bryce, I've been so worried. . . ."

Through the bandages a muffled voice replied, "It's over now, Claudine. There's no need to worry anymore."

His voice was so soft and different sounding. The bandages made it hardly recognizable. Claudine stared at him hesitantly.

"Could you take your glasses off? Just for a moment. Please?"

He hesitated for a moment, then, with his left hand, lifted them from his face. His expression was one of intense curiosity and surprise, as if he were seeing her for the first time. Close up she could see no sign of the hardness that had upset her before. Rather, his eyes seemed to express a sort of pity.

"Poor Claudine," he murmured.

A flood of emotions swept over her. Feelings of compassion, admiration for his courage and also a strange, new, undefinable emotion. She was at a loss for words and, careful not to give him the wrong impression, hid her confusion by putting his glasses back on him and smiling.

She took his left hand in hers and looked at it. There was a strip of bandage around his thumb, and scar lines replaced the usual creases on the palm of his hand.

"I hope you aren't too uncomfortable at the hotel," Bryce said in his new soft voice.

"I'm all right," Claudine assured him. She wondered how best to tell him about the boutique. Finally she decided to be straightforward. "I sold the boutique, Bryce. Mr. Charreau said he was keeping your position open for you and that we would probably be in Autun for quite a while. I thought it was best just to sell it rather than worry about trying to find someone to look after it the whole time."

She described to him the details of the sale, trying to determine what his reaction was. But with the bandages and glasses it was like talking to a mask. It was impossible to gauge the effect the news was having on him.

When she finished he was silent for a moment. "You shouldn't have sold it," he finally murmured.

Claudine was astounded. "Surely you don't mean that—after all you said about it before!"

This time there was an even longer silence.

"I've changed, Claudine."

Claudine didn't know what to say. Fortunately the nurse came in right then.

"That's enough for the first day," she said. "You can come back again tomorrow."

Claudine held his hand tenderly.

"See you again tomorrow, my love," Bryce said softly.

In the corridor the nurse watched Claudine, carefully trying to judge her reactions.

"Well?" she asked.

"I didn't recognize his voice or his hands."

"There was extensive surgery done on his hands. And he has to be very careful not to strain his vocal cords for some time yet. You can see him every day if you like, providing you don't talk to him for too long because he tires very quickly. Don't talk to him about the accident, and try to entertain him."

Claudine listened to the nurse's explanations, but her mind was on another change in Bryce, one that wasn't merely a matter of surgery. He had never before used endearments and now he was suddenly calling her "my love." She wondered if this was a sign of anxiety. Dr. Leroux had talked about a period of learning for Bryce, but Claudine was finding that she, too, had some learning to do.

They established a new routine. She anxiously awaited every visit. Bryce spoke very little, and in low tones, using abrupt phrases. There was no way for Claudine to find out how he felt about his condition. Whenever she even accidentally referred to his injuries, Bryce would stop her with a wave of his hand, the only humorous gesture he would allow himself.

Every time she saw him, Claudine realized more acutely how much Bryce had changed. Where he used to be impulsive, now he was patient. Indifference had been replaced by kindness. Often he would just sit quietly and hold her hand. Whenever he took off his dark glasses his expression was one of both gentle pity and anxious interrogation. He seemed to be asking something of her. What was he so afraid of?

Claudine was baffled. She had been expecting completely different behavior and was beginning to understand what he meant when he said he had changed. But to what extent? The only way she would find out would be to see him without the bandages that concealed his new face.

She didn't want to force any confidences from him, and since she had to avoid the subject that mattered most to her, she had to be satisfied with telling him the minute details of her daily life, describing the book she was reading or discussing television programs. The slightest effort exhausted him and he often fell into a doze when she was with him.

By now he was able to get up and sit in an armchair for several hours at a time with a blanket around his knees. He had lost so much weight that when he stood up he seemed taller. The only part of him that was visible was his left hand. The rest of his body was covered by either his bathrobe or bandages. The nerves of his right hand had been damaged, and it wasn't certain whether he would ever be able to use it again.

The president of his company and some of his colleagues came to visit. He was happy to receive them, though glad of the shelter of his bandages. He was sorry William had been detained in Paris and had been unable to return.

Claudine would read him the many letters they received. One had arrived from Canada from his sister, who had heard of the accident and was apparently ready to show Claudine some family solidarity.

"What on earth's got into her?" Bryce grumbled. "She doesn't even know you."

"I'm your wife. Maybe that's enough."

"Hmph! Dominique and her sentimentality!"

There had never been any affection between Bryce and his sister. As she had explained to Dr. Leroux, the children of the first wife had found it difficult to accept the second marriage. Dominique, who had been eleven at the time, had made it her business to turn her little brother, Christopher, who was seven years younger, against their "new mother." Bryce's birth and his mother's obvious preference for him did nothing to improve relations within the family. When she reached eighteen Dominique married a Canadian, and when their father died, Christopher, in turn, left home. At the age of twelve Bryce had been left with his mother, who had continued to spoil him outrageously.

So it was surprising for Dominique to be showing such sympathy all of a sudden. Bryce seemed to think it was a silly gesture, but Claudine was rather touched.

Chapter 5

November was drawing to a close. Snow fell in the valley and suddenly it was cold. Dr. Leroux was due back from the Caribbean in a few days, but the professor decided to send Bryce to a convalescent home at Brunoy, near Paris, without waiting for his assistant to return.

"The sooner he gets back to normal life, the better for him. At Brunoy he will be able to renew regular contact with the colleagues he's been working with and follow up on his research without interrupting his treatment. He'll have a physiotherapist and a speech therapist and, most important of all, a psychotherapist. He suffered no brain damage and has no trouble with his memory or perception, but a shock such as this leaves scars, and the most pernicious are those we can't see."

"How long will he have to stay at Brunoy?" Claudine asked.

"A month or two, depending on his general condition." The professor hesitated. "By the way, he still doesn't want you to see him without bandages and he made me promise to wait until you had left Mountain Spring before I had them removed."

"Are the scars very terrible?"

"Not at all. He has a phobia about them, which is completely unjustified. Here, you can judge for yourself. I've taken a photograph of him. He thinks it's strictly for medical records, so I trust you not to give me away."

Claudine reached out eagerly and grasped the photograph he was holding out to her.

She had had so many fears, had so much expected the worst, that she was filled with indescribable joy and relief when she saw the face in the photo. Although it wasn't the Bryce that she remembered, it was a normal, very attractive face, and some of the features were surprisingly familiar. Dr. Leroux had warned her so often not to expect any similarities to the original that Claudine could see some that she might otherwise have missed. His chin, the shape of his mouth, his forehead, they were all familiar. Even the hairline was the same, although his hair had had to be shaved and was only just beginning to grow again. Every feature had changed, but the face in the photograph bore at least something of a family resemblance to the one she remembered.

"Reassured?" asked the professor.

"It's much, much better than I ever dared hope. I can't tell you what I feared!"

"So you doubted us? You shouldn't have. We are the magicians of our era. Soon people will be able to choose their faces out of catalogs."

She thanked him effusively for bringing the photograph.

He took the picture back, smiling. "Dr. Leroux wanted to wait and show you the completed masterpiece. I don't have his author's vanity."

"Can I keep the photograph?"

"I'm sorry. I've already transgressed professional ethics by showing it to you without the patient's consent."

The picture had so relieved Claudine that she was still beaming when she walked into Bryce's room later that day.

"You look happy," he commented.

"I've heard we'll be leaving here soon. I think we're beginning to see the light at the end of the passage."

His hand tightened on the arm of the chair and he said, so softly that she could barely hear him, "The end of the passage? Poor Claudine."

"Aren't you pleased to be leaving?" she asked.

"I don't know."

Having just seen the photograph, Claudine couldn't understand why Bryce insisted on hiding his face. Still filled with uncertainty, Claudine's mind concocted a new fear. Perhaps his features had lost their mobility. She remembered seeing an actor who had been in a severe accident and had had plastic surgery, which left his face strangely rigid. Perhaps this was Bryce's secret fear. Claudine asked the professor about this.

"No, I would have let you know if that had been the case. At this stage it would be cruel to hide anything from you. I'm only letting your husband leave because I'm certain he won't suffer any physical repercussions from the accident. My only concern is that there might be psychological problems. You'll have to watch out for that, but if I were in your position I would be thanking God for the recovery he's made. You should have seen the first X rays. Leroux has worked miracles."

The professor looked a bit gloomy and for a moment Claudine was amused by the idea that he might be a little jealous of his assistant.

Bryce was to make the journey to Brunoy by ambulance, accompanied by Lucy, his nurse. The evening before his departure, Claudine took leave of the guests in the hotel and the people in the village who had been so kind to her.

Leaving Villars-les-Saint-Pierre for the last time, Claudine sat in the taxi looking out the window at the snow-covered valley. She was suddenly filled with an inexplicable melancholy. All the weeks of pain and worry and heartache since the mysterious accident were behind her now. But what did it all mean? And what did the future hold?

She looked out of the frosty window but all she could see was the strange, pitying look in Bryce's eyes as he had murmured, as if in warning, "Poor Claudine."

THE CONVALESCENT HOME AT BRUNOY was located in a luxurious, old-fashioned château. It was placed in the middle of a huge park that would be beautiful in summer. But the bare, leafless trees and frozen ground of winter gave the place a slightly sinister feeling.

Inside the château it was warm and cheerful. Bryce had a spacious, airy room on the top floor. It had large windows and was furnished more like a hotel than a clinic.

Bryce was in the hands of three specialists: a

physiotherapist to make his limbs work again, a
speech therapist to retrain his vocal cords and, finally, a psychotherapist. The latter, Dr. Laurent, was as
interested in Claudine as he was in Bryce. Very soon
after Bryce's transfer, he called her to his office in
Paris to give her some warning of what was to come.
Bryce was still in a state of shock, he told her, and his
recovery depended largely on Claudine's understanding. He was insisting on wearing bandages, although
he didn't need them, because he wanted to get used to
his new features himself before he showed them to
her.

Although Claudine tried to be sympathetic to
Bryce's fears, she couldn't help feeling impatient for
the day when he'd take the bandages off.

Bryce was steadily learning to live again. His
body, which had been immobile for so long, was
slowly rediscovering its ability to move. Despite the
gloomy weather he walked a little farther in the park
each day and he exercised his right hand for hours at
a time, but without much result. His voice developed
to normal strength, though it was not, and never
would be, the same.

His friends wanted to come and visit him, but
Bryce said that he was too tired to see all of them. Instead, he spent several hours each day with his colleagues from work who brought him large files,
which they went through together.

"This is all so fascinating," he said enthusiastically
to Claudine, indicating the open files. "I can't wait to
get back."

She glanced over the pages, which were covered
with long equations. "It doesn't look fascinating!"

"No, I suppose it doesn't, to the uninitiated. But

look, what we're doing here is creating a synthetic fuel additive. If we succeed, we could cut our consumption of oil by nearly half. The possibilities of this research are staggering."

Claudine looked more closely at the papers, more impressed than she had been before. She had never had any idea of what Bryce's research involved.

"And the reason that we have to build the new laboratories," he continued, "is that we need a special kind of control chamber."

Claudine listened with pleased interest. Bryce had never discussed his work with her before. She was delighted that he now seemed to want to share it with her.

Bryce looked at her and was silent for a moment. "I'm sorry. This must be boring you."

"Not at all," Claudine assured him. "I enjoy hearing about your work."

"Poor Claudine. You must be getting tired of having to come here every day and sit with me. I really don't expect you to, you know."

"What do you mean?" Claudine was slightly taken aback. "Of course I'm going to come visit you every day!"

"But I know what a bother it must be. You really don't have to do all this. I'll understand."

Claudine couldn't help but be somewhat skeptical of these kind thoughts that were so little like the inconsiderate Bryce of old. Suspecting sarcasm, she replied crisply, "If my visits are tiring you, Bryce, please say so."

"Don't be ridiculous. You know that it's only because of you that I've made it through this ordeal. Your visits are about the only bright point in my entire day. I was just thinking that you probably have a lot of things you would like to do in Paris."

"Well, I really haven't got all that much to do since I've sold the boutique."

"Yes, it's too bad that you sold it. If I had known what you were doing I would have advised you against it. I'm afraid that you might start feeling too tied down now without it."

"Oh, I can always sew," she replied hesitantly. For a moment she gazed at him searchingly, wondering what could have caused such a remarkable change of heart. It was almost as if Bryce didn't remember how many times he had argued with her, trying to get her to give up her work. She felt quite unnerved.

BACK IN THEIR PARIS APARTMENT, Claudine began to wonder if perhaps Bryce's memory had been affected by the accident. She decided to call the clinic at Mountain Spring to find out what Dr. Leroux's opinion was of the possibility of amnesia.

"Leroux isn't back yet," the professor informed her. "Maybe I can be of help."

"I'm really afraid Bryce's memory has been harmed," she told him.

"Absolutely not. The tests have definitely proved otherwise. He might forget details, but which of us doesn't do that?"

Claudine explained about the boutique and said that she didn't think that an area of conflict that had almost wrecked their marriage could be considered a detail.

"Possibly," the professor replied after listening to her carefully, "possibly Bryce just wishes to efface all his bad memories. Trying to wipe the old slate clean, so to speak."

Remembering how Bryce had all his photographs destroyed, Claudine found this explanation more acceptable. She decided that if Bryce wanted to forget all the bad things in their past she would go along with him and would make a point of not mentioning their old arguments or areas of contention.

Bryce's continuing kindness rekindled feelings in Claudine that she had thought had died forever. It was almost like the first few weeks she had known him. But it wasn't the same blind adoration, it was a deeper, more intense attachment. These feelings bothered Claudine as she remembered how she had deceived herself the first time. She reminded herself that Bryce was still convalescing, his wounds not yet healed, and he hadn't had time to forget how close he had been to death. When the impact of his ordeal had faded a little and they once again began to live a normal life together, with its inevitable monotonies and disagreements, his old, difficult personality might reassert itself.

For the moment, however, she took advantage of the new Bryce, who called her "my love" and took an interest in her. He had always before been bored by stories of her childhood and teens, but now he asked innumerable questions about her family and her friends. He seemed to like her to reminisce about the way they had met, their short engagement and the few pleasures they had shared, as if he regretted not having given enough importance to those few, fleeting hours that might have been his last.

Since Bryce continued to avoid any mention of their disagreements, Claudine did so, as well. He seemed happy enough to talk about his childhood, with a wealth of detail that proved his memory was undamaged. He told her what he had been like when he was a little boy, and Claudine heard many stories for the first time. Curiously, he talked mostly about his father, who had died early in his life, rarely mentioning his mother with whom he had lived for a long time.

Christmas was drawing near. This would be their second Christmas together and Claudine felt that they were closer than they had been throughout their marriage. Bryce was extremely anxious to recover quickly and he worried that the laboratories at Autun would be finished before he left the clinic. Both the doctors and his employer reassured him. Construction wouldn't be completed until the spring, and Bryce would be active again long before then.

ONE MORNING, as Claudine was about to leave the apartment to do some errands, the phone rang.

"Is that you, Claudine?"

It was Bryce, but it was the first time that Claudine had talked to him on the phone since the accident. His voice was different yet something about it was almost hauntingly familiar.

"Are you there, Claudine? I'm calling from Brunoy. Didn't you recognize my voice?"

"Yes, I was just surprised. Is everything all right?"

"I just wanted to warn you that I've had the bandages removed. For good. I wanted you to be prepared."

Claudine was uncertain of what to say. She had been waiting so long for this moment, and yet now it seemed so sudden.

"I've been preparing for it, Bryce. Please don't worry."

"All right. I just wanted to make sure. I'll see you soon, my love."

There was no longer any thought of errands. Claudine called a taxi immediately and sped to the clinic. Her heart was beating wildly. The moment had come at last. Bryce had sounded so fearful. Claudine had prepared words for this occasion, but suddenly they seemed inadequate.

Bryce was pacing up and down in his room when she arrived. He was dressed in slacks and a pullover he had borrowed from William. He turned abruptly toward her, his features taut with anxiety. Claudine stopped, suddenly shy, and looked at him.

His face was even better than the photograph. His hair had grown back. It was curlier and darker than previously, but it still had the same gold highlights. She had to look hard to see any sign at àll of the surgery. There were a few small scars on the edge of his hairline and behind his ears. Only the one fine line running down the length of his neck was obvious. His dark eyes were both familiar yet completely different.

He didn't look like the old Bryce. He looked like a man who had faced a test of moral strength. He had rather ascetic features and a more serious expression on his face. He had completely lost the look of a petulant, spoiled child that he used to have. But none of that mattered to Claudine. All that was important to her was that he was alive and that he wouldn't be disfigured or an invalid.

Claudine felt so relieved and the agitation on Bryce's features seemed so out of place that she had to laugh.

"Bryce, you look fantastic!"

He smiled wryly. "It could be worse."

"But, Bryce, it's amazing! You look much better than you did before." The words had tumbled out spontaneously and Claudine immediately regretted them.

"You were really afraid?" he asked.

"Weren't you?"

He stared at her intensely, his eyes full of concern. "I'm just beginning to be afraid," he said finally.

Chapter 6

Now that his bandages were off, Bryce became even more self-conscious about receiving visitors. He didn't even want to see his colleagues with whom he had enjoyed talking. This reluctance began to worry Claudine and she asked Bryce's psychotherapist about it.

Dr. Laurent assured her that there was nothing unusual about such a reaction. He explained that many of the burns had left ugly scars on Bryce's body, and even though these scars couldn't be seen by the visitors, Bryce felt shame and rejection toward his face and body. The doctor counseled patience, saying that in time Bryce would become less self-conscious.

Claudine still found Bryce's hesitancy hard to understand. To her, Bryce really did look better than before. Dr. Leroux had indeed attained perfect results. Like a procelain repairer with a delicate vase, who repaints and revarnishes until even the keenest eye can no longer discern the breaks, he had achieved perfection. All that was missing was the resemblance to the old Bryce.

Claudine was willing to let Bryce move at his own pace. But William had called four or five times and each time had been turned away. Claudine finally prevailed on Bryce to let his old friend visit.

That day she had lunch with Bryce in his room. He was tired and hadn't got up, and throughout lunch he kept looking nervously toward the door.

"William's late. Are you sure he's coming today?" he asked at one point.

"Absolutely certain. Don't forget it's Saturday, and the roads are probably very slow. You're awfully impatient."

"I'm sorry, dear." He smiled. "This isn't an occasion I'm looking forward to and I'd like to get it over with. I don't think I would be able to get through it if it weren't for you."

There was a knock at the door. Bryce's expression hardened. William opened the door and stood there, motionless, incapable of hiding his shock.

"It's fantastic! Unbelievable! I never imagined it would be so successful!" William gasped.

Claudine stiffened. She should have known that despite all her warnings to be careful, William would blurt out something tactless. Tensely she watched Bryce, waiting for the negative reaction she expected to come..

"I hope you aren't going to say you wouldn't have recognized me."

"Well, almost!"

Suddenly Bryce relaxed and they both started to laugh. Greatly relieved, Claudine watched them talking for a while and then left them to themselves and went out to walk in the park.

The bare trees and dim white sky immediately made Claudine feel depressed and tired. She stuck her hands deep into the felt-lined pockets of her coat and walked down the cold paths, her breath misting in the frosty air. The continual emotional strain was beginning to wear her down. Why did that strange, unexplained accident ever have to happen? She felt almost guilty for thinking that. After all, he could so easily have died or been disfigured and crippled. She told herself that she should be continually thankful. Still, she felt she couldn't wait until things got back to normal.

The thought made her stop and shake her head. What was she thinking of—things were never going to be the way they were before. Nothing was going to be normal anymore. She had traded in her old life for something new.

She walked along, feeling the cold in her cheeks and on her nose, trying to understand what this new life was. Bryce was so different, so kind and gentle, so much more considerate than he had been before. Yet there was some new inner strength in him, as well. It was as if there were some great, powerful purpose burning steadfastly deep within him. He seemed to have grown so much older and more experienced, like a man who's been on a long, dangerous journey. His childish habits had been trimmed away, and though the ordeal seemed to have left him much kinder, it also seemed to have made him in some way more determined.

Claudine realized that she could no longer tell what her husband was thinking or what his feelings were about her or the things that were going on. She even felt a tremor of excitement when thinking how affectionate he was to her now. It was like being married to the most seductive of strangers.

Claudine suddenly shuddered. It was just the chill in the air, she told herself, turning back toward the clinic.

William had already left by the time Claudine returned. Bryce seemed to be more relaxed than he had been before the visit. He smiled as she entered the room.

"How did it go?" she asked. "Was it very bad?"

"No. The first few minutes were kind of rough. But after that it went all right. But I must say, as much as I like William, he is rather rude and inconsiderate. Some of his remarks were quite embarrassing."

"That's a switch!" Claudine remarked with surprise.

"What do you mean? Don't you agree?"

"You know I've never cared for him. I've always thought that he was untrustworthy. You're the one who always excused his inconsiderate remarks."

"Anyway—" Bryce paused for a moment, then went on "—at least now I feel a little easier about seeing people. William was the hardest and now that that's done, it won't be so difficult to see the others."

Claudine sat down next to him on the edge of his bed. "I'm glad to hear that. I was getting worried. I realize how hard this is for you, but it seems to me that the sooner we get these things over with, the sooner we can start living a normal life again."

She gently took hold of his left hand while talking and caressed the scars along his palm. She looked up to see Bryce staring at her as if somehow surprised.

After a minute he drew his hand back and shook his head as if to clear it of some thought that didn't belong there.

"I've got a lot of work to do now," he said almost gruffly. "You'd better run along."

Surprised and somewhat hurt by his sudden change in manner, Claudine kissed him lightly and left, filled again with confusion.

A FEW DAYS LATER Claudine had a date to meet with her friend Sophie. Sophie had insisted on taking her out shopping in order to try to get Claudine to forget about her worries for a little while at least.

Since the day was cold and wet, Claudine dressed warmly in a dark blue wool skirt and a scarlet wool sweater. Because of the possibility of rain she wore high boots and her navy trench coat and matching hat.

Outside, a thin drizzle was falling over everything. Dark tree branches hung limply over the gray sodden streets. Here and there a pedestrian hurried along, head bent and shoulders hunched against the drizzle, intent only on reaching a dry destination.

Claudine regretted not having taken a taxi to Sophie's. She buttoned her coat and turned the collar up. She walked quickly, huddling close to the sides of buildings, hypnotized by the reflections of the passing cars, which gleamed darkly on the wet roads in the dim winter afternoon.

By the time she got to Sophie's, Claudine was no longer in any mood to go shopping. Sophie invited her in and sat her next to the radiator while she fixed some hot chocolate and rolls.

"This weather's enough to get anyone down," Sophie said cheerfully, handing her a steaming mug.

"I know, and I'm sorry, Sophie. I really did want to go shopping and have a good time."

"Don't worry about it. We'll have fun right here. I haven't had much of a chance to talk to you lately."

Claudine sipped her hot chocolate and felt its warmth gradually driving the chill from her. "I'm out at the clinic almost every day. And at night I'm usually so tired and worn out that it's the best I can do just to have a bath and go to bed. It's funny how much energy it takes simply to worry!"

"Poor Claudine, I know how you must feel. Is Bryce giving you a hard time?"

"What do you mean?"

"Oh, just that from what you've told me of Bryce, I guess he must complain all the time and make things pretty miserable for you."

"No, not at all." Claudine smiled, remembering how the old Bryce would complain incessantly about even the slightest cold. "That's the funny part about it. If it weren't for his kindness, his courage in the face of all this, I don't think I would really find the strength to get through. But when I see how well he's taking it, with all the pain and suffering he has been going through, it makes me feel as if I can do it, too."

Sophie looked at her, puzzled and confused.

"Bryce has changed," Claudine continued, responding to her friend's expression. "He's much different from before. He doesn't complain at all. And his only concern seems to be for my welfare."

"Are you sure we're talking about the same person?"

Claudine laughed. "I know it's hard to believe, but

he's changed. He came very close to dying, you know. I guess the experience of that can really change a person."

"I'm sure it's quite an affecting experience," Sophie agreed, somewhat dryly. "But how long do you think a change like that will last?"

"I don't know, Sophie, it's hard to explain. He really is different. It's not just a matter of being polite. There's something in him, deep down, something new."

Sophie looked at the intensity on her friend's face and shook her head. "So how did the plastic surgery turn out?" she asked, changing the subject.

"Just incredible. You wouldn't believe how good a job they did. He looks completely different, but you can hardly see any signs at all of the surgery."

"Has it changed his looks very much?"

"Completely! If you met him on the street you wouldn't recognize him. They've changed every one of his features. And he's even better looking than he was before."

Sophie laughed and went out to the kitchen to get some more rolls.

"Do you regret having sold your boutique?" she asked curiously when she returned.

"I miss it a little," Claudine conceded. "But I think I did the right thing in selling it. I really wouldn't have the time to look after it now."

"I suppose that Bryce is happier that you did."

"As a matter of fact, he isn't. Now he says that he wishes I hadn't sold it."

Sophie raised her eyebrows eloquently. "Well, I guess he has changed. It's strange—you'd think that being laid up for so long would have made him

crankier than he was. At any other time he would
have become more bitter and demanding. Instead,
you say he's become kind and understanding. I guess
a close brush with death really does something to a
person."

Claudine agreed. But later that night, as she was
preparing for bed, she found herself wondering. Just
what had the experience done to Bryce?

CHRISTMAS CAME. As a celebration, Claudine prepared a dinner for her and Bryce to have in his room.
She wanted to do something special, so she made it as
elegant as she could. Along with the food, which she
had cooked at home, she brought a lace tablecloth,
wine and even candles. She spent nearly as much
time in getting dressed as she had in cooking the
food. She wore a brand-new peach-colored evening
gown. It was cut very low in the front and was slit up
one side to the hip. She would have been too self-
conscious to wear it in public and had bought it sole-
ly for this occasion when she would be alone with
Bryce. She twisted her glossy dark brown hair on top
of her head, setting off to advantage her white shoulders and the delicate lines of her chin and throat.
Only a touch of makeup was necessary to enhance
her wide, dark eyes and fair-skinned freshness.

None of this was lost on Bryce, whose eyes never
left her as she set up the table and served the
meal. His gaze was so intense and ardent that Claudine was amazed to find herself blushing. She felt as
flustered and hesitant as a schoolgirl and hardly
knew how to reply to Bryce's charming conversation
as they ate.

"Dominique says that she'll be visiting us this sum-

Chapter 7

Bryce was going to have to get used to his new body and all the changes that had been made. His stay at Brunoy was drawing to a close, yet he was still uneasy with visitors and refused to see all their friends. He said he felt too much like a curiosity, as if he were some kind of freak in a side-show.

Bryce's psychotherapist, Dr. Laurent, said his reactions were quite normal and that Claudine should just be patient. It took him time to make such a big adjustment.

Claudine was still worried and decided to call Dr. Leroux at the Mountain Spring Clinic to see what he would advise. But when Claudine called the clinic, she was told that, for personal reasons, Leroux had to extend his leave and it wasn't known when, or if, he'd return.

The doctors at Brunoy had decided to release Bryce at the end of February. The latest reports on his health had been excellent and the only remaining physical marks of his accident would be his scars and a partial paralysis of his right hand.

Still, after having been in the hospital for six months, there was no possibility of his going directly back to work. The doctors wanted him to take a month's holiday, but Bryce was so anxious to get back to the labs that they agreed to three weeks, provided that he spent two of those weeks in the sun.

In order to find some sun they were going to have to travel. Bryce suggested that they go to Amalfi, and since she had never been to Italy, Claudine agreed enthusiastically.

Before they left the hospital, Dr. Laurent called Claudine into his office to give her some final pieces of advice.

"You mustn't judge by appearances," he began. "Your husband's body has done a good job of mending itself, and there is no possibility of any physical infirmity. But his psyche hasn't mended itself as quickly. The accident will probably affect his behavior for some time. He's still obsessed with his scars and you shouldn't treat this obsession lightly. He hasn't come to terms with his new identity yet."

The doctor seemed hesitant and Claudine looked at him questioningly.

"What I'm trying to say is that you should be prepared for him to want to keep some distance between you. He may even want you to have separate bedrooms and you shouldn't press him to have full marital relations until he is ready. The initiative must come from him or the consequences could be disastrous."

Claudine flushed. She knew that Bryce wasn't completely over the effects of the accident yet, but she hadn't realized that the shock would be that extreme.

"What do you think would happen?" she asked.

"He could have a nervous breakdown, or a lasting psychosis. I realize it isn't fair to ask a young woman such as yourself to give up her sex life, but it will be only temporary and your husband's health is at stake."

The choice was clear, and as Claudine left the doctor's office she was surprised to find that mixed in with her disappointment was a sense of relief. She realized that Bryce was so different from his old self that she had been somewhat intimidated by the idea of renewing their intimacy. His phobia could, in fact, be advantageous, because it would give them time to get to know each other again.

Before they could go to Amalfi they had business to settle in Paris. Bryce had to get new identification papers and some of his clothes, which were now too loose, had to be taken to the tailor to be altered.

For Bryce, returning to the apartment was an ordeal. It was going to be impossible to escape the scrutiny of the superintendent and the neighbors, whose sympathy and intrusive questions were something that he was not at all looking forward to.

When Claudine saw him in their apartment for the first time since the accident, she was suddenly fearful. It was as if the familiar surroundings emphasized the change in him. She wondered if he felt the same way. He avoided the mirrors and looked around attentively, like a man returning from a long journey and finding that his memory had distorted the most commonplace articles.

Claudine had taken great care in tidying and arranging the apartment for his homecoming and had bought bright spring flowers and arranged them in vases scattered around the living room and bedroom.

"It's pretty here," he said softly.

"Had you forgotten?"

"I'd stopped noticing." He walked over to the window and looked out at the trees in the square. "I didn't get to see the autumn," he said turning around and smiling at her. "You bought flowers. It's like a celebration."

"It *is* a celebration."

"It's...a beginning. The beginning of a long road strewn with snares." With a weary gesture he sank into the armchair that Claudine always used.

"And for a start, you're taking my place," she teased.

He looked baffled and Claudine immediately regretted the remark.

"You must be tired, Bryce. Shall I make your bed up for you?"

"No, I'd like to go out. Let's eat in a restaurant. Not locally. I'd like to be somewhere where no one will pay any attention to me."

"We can go to the Saint-Germain-des-Prés district," Claudine suggested. "I know a good Italian restaurant on the rue des Canettes. Oh, sorry. I'd forgotten you can't bear Italian food."

"Tonight I'd love it! Gastronomically, the clinic left a lot to be desired."

In the subway Bryce observed the trains and the passengers like a man risen from the dead. It was as though either his close brush with death or his long period of immobilization had given the most day-to-day happenings an aura of novelty.

In the restaurant he ate well but spoke very little. Claudine was used to his silences, but now they had a special quality, and instead of dividing them they seemed to bring them closer together. All through the meal his eyes never left her.

Nearly all the tables were occupied. Through the babble of conversation going on around them, Claudine explained that she had often lunched there, since it was so close to her business.

"Do you miss the boutique?"

"No. Not yet."

"But it did make you more independent. I hope you aren't going to feel confined now."

Once again Claudine was impressed with his new thoughtfulness.

"I'm beginning to make some more outfits," Claudine said. In the past he had always ridiculed her craft, but now he took her hand.

"Thank you, my love, for all you are doing for me. I appreciate the sacrifice it must be for you."

After dinner he wanted to walk. The temperature had risen over the last few days, and even though it was just the beginning of March, it almost felt like spring. There were lots of people strolling on the sidewalk.

A man of about forty with long hair and a beard walked toward Bryce, his hand outstretched in greeting.

"Chevalier! How are you?"

Bryce looked startled. "Hello there, Marnier. Excuse us, we're in a hurry."

Without stopping, Bryce hustled Claudine toward the nearest taxi.

"Get in," he ordered. "Quick."

He looked back nervously as the taxi pulled away.

"Why did you rush off like that?"

"The man's a sponger. I don't want to associate with him."

Claudine was puzzled about why this slightly unpleasant incident had upset Bryce so much. All the way back to the apartment he sat silent and frowning.

CLAUDINE HAD WANTED Bryce to take the bedroom, but he refused, and she had to let him sleep on a divan in the living room. In the back of her mind, however, she hoped that this arrangement would prove so uncomfortable that he would decide to move back into the bedroom. But Dr. Laurent was right. Bryce didn't want her to see his body and he took unbelievable precautions to ensure that she didn't.

The next morning he was up and dressed before Claudine emerged from the bedroom.

She scolded him for getting up first. "I wanted to give you breakfast in bed!"

"I'd rather have it with you in the kitchen," he replied.

Another change. He had always insisted before on having his coffee in the living room while he read the morning paper. Claudine put two coffee cups on the kitchen table, slightly disconcerted by the novelty of a morning tête-à-tête with her husband.

"You can read your paper if you want to," she assured him anxiously.

"I can do that later. After all, I'm on a vacation." He smiled. "The coffee's very good," he added.

Claudine felt slightly embarrassed by all his kind

attention. He was trying so hard to be nice to her; she wanted to make it easier for him.

"You're being very sweet, Bryce, and I appreciate it. But you don't have to compliment everything I do, you know."

The shocked look on his face told her immediately that she had made a mistake. He was right, there were a lot of snares on their road.

BRYCE OBTAINED HIS PAPERS in record time. His identity card carried exactly the same information as it had before: age, height, color of eyes and hair. But when Claudine saw the photograph and his clumsy left-handed signature, she felt as if another link with their past had been broken.

A few days later they arrived in Amalfi in the pouring rain. They rented a car at the airport and Claudine drove along the winding coastal road. She drove slowly, but the road was slick and the car skidded several times. It was a relief when they finally reached their destination.

The wonderful hotel where Bryce had reserved rooms had formerly been a Franciscan monastery. It was built into the side of a hill so steep that the only way to reach it was by an elevator that ran down the cliff face. It had interminable corridors broken by long staircases, elegant eighteenth-century furniture and balconies overlooking the sea.

Claudine had never stayed in such a luxurious hotel and she was ecstatic. Everything was so beautiful. But she was worried about whether Bryce was going to enjoy himself, whether he would be bored now that he was forbidden all sports.

Claudine was slightly disconcerted when she found

that Bryce had reserved two separate rooms. She helped him unpack and put away the two new suits he had bought because the tailor hadn't been able to complete the alterations to the old ones in time. He watched her as she moved around the room, and when she had finished he took her hand and raised it to his lips.

"Poor Claudine. These last few months must have been terrible for you."

Without thinking, Claudine threw her arms around his neck and impulsively kissed him. Too late, she realized that he had tensed. She felt him draw back, then he lifted her arms down and gently pushed her away.

"I'm tired from the journey," he said. "I'm going to go to sleep until dinner. Why don't you settle yourself in?"

He was virtually throwing her out! Pained and humiliated, she started to protest but stopped herself in time, remembering what the psychotherapist had said. Struggling with her inner turmoil, Claudine forced herself to smile.

"Of course you're tired, Bryce. You rest. I'll call you in time for dinner."

Uncertain of how much of her feelings she had revealed, Claudine went to her own room and closed the door gently behind her. She took a few minutes to calm down, reminding herself how important it was to let Bryce take his time, and how much it would probably hurt him if he felt her impatience. As she dressed for dinner she wondered how long her naturally impetuous nature would allow her to give Bryce the patient understanding that he needed.

The rooms were well-heated, but afraid that the

corridors would be drafty, Claudine dressed warmly in a crimson wool djeliaba that she had designed recently and that Bryce hadn't seen. By the time she went to call him for dinner he had changed, too. His velvet suit was very becoming, though not quite in the same mode as the "company director" image he had always liked to portray.

"I like your suit, Bryce. It's not quite the same style as your others, though."

"I needed a new look," he said, then laughed.

Claudine was surprised at the joke, but she was pleased that he was able to laugh about it. Maybe it was a sign of his becoming more comfortable with his changed appearance.

The restaurant was in a large room with tall arched windows through which nothing could be seen except the downpouring rain. As he seated them, the maître d' assured them that the view was magnificent. Usually.

The atmosphere was very romantic. On the tables there were candles burning, and small vases held charming arrangements of local flowers. There were many guests in the hotel, even though it was out of season. There were elderly people chasing the sun, younger couples, Germans, Scandinavians.

In the flickering candlelight, guests and surroundings were punctuated by warm, dancing shadows. Bryce looked across the table, his eyes twinkling.

"If one of our friends from before came into the room now he would think you were having an affair."

Claudine felt a warm blush creep up her neck and tint her cheeks. The other guests probably did take them for honeymooners. Especially if they judged by the ardent expression in Bryce's eyes and the tenderness in his voice.

Claudine felt almost dizzy with love. The emotion was so strong, so unlike anything she had ever felt before, that her knees were weak from the force of it. Maybe they could begin again. Perhaps they could start all over and forget about all that they had gone through, all the arguments and disagreements, all the pain and heartache.

Claudine lifted her wineglass and, in a voice that trembled slightly, toasted Bryce.

"To your recovery."

Bryce's eyes looked deep into hers as he lifted his glass in return.

"To our futures."

It wasn't until much later that Claudine was struck by the peculiarity of his toast.

Chapter 8

Alone in her dark room, the rain pounding against the ancient slate roof, Claudine lay on her bed, her face buried in her arms, trying to keep back the tears that threatened to overpower her.

The evening had been so perfect, and Bryce had seemed so close and so affectionate that Claudine's emotions had got the better of her and she had convinced herself that Bryce was going to overcome his complexes and spend the night with her. She had felt more in love with him than she had ever felt before. But at the end of the evening he had walked her to her door, kissed her hand gently and bidden her good-night.

The romantic, luxurious atmosphere made her feel lonelier than she had ever felt in her whole life. She fought against the tears, telling herself to be patient, that everything would work out if she just gave it time. She knew that if she didn't give Bryce the understanding that he needed, that if she tried to push things ahead faster than he could go, it would

all end in disaster. She bit her lip to keep it from
trembling and tried to think only of how far they had
already come. She thought of Bryce's gentle touch
and that look in his eyes of some deep and secret
pain.

She fought as hard as she could against her tears,
but the desolate sound of the rain falling in the long
black night was too much. By the time Claudine fell
wearily to sleep her pillow was soaked.

THE NEXT MORNING it was too sunny to be sad. Overnight the storm had disappeared and was replaced by
brilliant Italian sunlight. Under the fresh sky a
magnificent vista of rugged mountains fell away
steeply toward an unbelievably clear and sparkling
blue sea. Claudine's window looked out over a ter-
raced garden overflowing with brightly colored giant
camellias, Japanese plum trees and mimosa.

In the bright morning sunlight the previous night's
tears seemed foolish. Claudine felt that the long
nightmare of pain and travail that their marriage had
gone through was over. Though badly begun, their
marriage could still be a success. Under the auspices
of the blue morning sky anything seemed possible.

Bryce was waiting for her under the arches of the
cloister. He didn't see her approach and she took advantage of the opportunity to look at him closely. He
was wearing a long-sleeved shirt, with an open neck
and a scarf. The sleeves covered the scars on his
wrist, just as his curly hair hid those on his temples.
The only mark that showed was the one that ran in a
single line down his neck. His strong profile was
clearly defined against the blue of the sky. Claudine
was once again struck by how handsome he was.

Quietly she walked up to him, slipped her arm through his and, looking out at the landscape, remarked softly, "It's beautiful, isn't it?"

"Beautiful," he replied. But he was looking at Claudine, not at the scenery. He stood like this for a few moments, then his expression changed and he looked away.

They spent that day and those that followed exploring the streets of the old town. Most of their time was spent together; the rest Bryce used to study the files of reports he had brought with him.

The nights were cold, but when the sun came out it was like summer. They hired a car and explored the villages along the coast, with their tiny white houses packed tightly together along the water's edge and magnificent old churches with frescoed cupolas. They went to Ravellow, which was about the same size as Amalfi, and they explored its magic gardens where, according to legend, the ghost of a flower girl wanders.

Claudine found it an enriching experience. She had never been to Italy before and had no idea of the magnificence of its historical and cultural wealth. Bryce was getting much stronger and they journeyed a little further each day. Together they explored Naples, Pompeii, Vesuvius and the Greek temples of Paestum lying sleepily alongside the Tyrrhenian Sea. Bryce was as enthusiastic as Claudine about their discoveries, most of the time laughing and happy. Claudine had never felt closer to pure joy.

But despite their happy companionship, Bryce kept the door between their rooms firmly closed. Claudine felt as if they were an old-fashioned courting couple under the strict eye of a chaperon. The most daring caress he allowed himself was an occasional fleeting kiss, and if she tried to get closer he slipped away on the slenderest of pretexts.

Often he seemed to be struggling against himself. He seemed to fight against the desire to show affection for her as one would fight against the desire to do something he knew wasn't right. Claudine couldn't understand this attitude, but as Bryce had grown quite sensitive to her questions, she was afraid to discuss it.

He didn't even want to talk about how he was adjusting to his new body. When Claudine asked him about the accident he told her he didn't remember anything about it, not even why he had been driving alone up on that narrow mountain road. Her questions seemed only to annoy him and she got no information whatever.

This new secretiveness depressed Claudine. She felt as if he didn't trust her. She even began to wonder if his kindness was really only indifference. Why did he seem to be sorry for her? What was it that he knew that made him pity her and call her "my poor Claudine"?

While Bryce worked in his room Claudine struggled alone with these questions. She began to think that perhaps Bryce had been embittered by their past and all their quarreling. Maybe he was only waiting until he was strong enough to leave her. Claudine was frustrated and confused and wasn't really sure what to think.

One evening, on their way back to their rooms after dinner, Claudine decided that she wanted to see the Gothic cloister. The moon shone down on the double row of narrow arches that reached skyward like joined hands. It was cool. She leaned closer to Bryce and his arm moved spontaneously around her shoulders. Then, bending his dark head, for the first time since the accident, he passionately kissed her. The kiss was so strong and ardent that it left Claudine breathless.

When he drew away there was a mixture of anger and desolation on his face.

"I'm sorry," he murmured.

"You're sorry? Bryce, I'm your wife!"

Without a word he turned and strode from the cloister so fast that Claudine could hardly keep up with him. At the main door of his room he stopped.

"Come inside, I owe you an explanation for all this," he said.

She went into the room and he helped her off with her coat.

"Please don't take this personally, Claudine. I want you to be my wife in every sense, but. . . didn't Dr. Laurent tell you?"

"I love you, Bryce."

He stood in front of her, putting his fingers under her chin and raising it as one does to a child one wants to scold but not frighten.

"I haven't forgotten anything, you know."

Claudine thought that he meant that he was still bitter about all the arguments they used to have.

"Neither have I, Bryce. I know we'd drawn a long way apart, and we argued bitterly and often. I thought our marriage was going to break up, and at first I stayed with you through a sense of guilt. But since then everything has changed."

"What are you talking about!" Bryce burst out in a shout.

"Our disagreements belong in the past," Claudine continued. "You're different from what you were, and I love you as you are now."

Bryce was looking at her aghast, almost with a look of terror on his face. Abruptly he turned away and leaned his forehead against the window. She didn't understand what she had said that could have upset him so much.

"Bryce? Are you all right?"

He turned back toward her. "You're right," he murmured, "I have changed. More than you think. I don't doubt your love at all, but at the moment it's your friendship I need."

"You don't love me anymore?" Her voice was strained.

He smiled gently. "Yes, I love you. More than I could have thought possible. But I beg you to give me more time...I can't show myself to you as I am."

"It doesn't matter to me, Bryce."

"I'm not so sure of that."

There was a suggestion in his words of a double meaning that she couldn't understand. She let him walk her back to her room.

That night she slept with the taste of his kiss on her lips. It felt as if he had kissed her for the first time.

THE RAIN CAME BACK. It dug deep furrows through the gardens and shattered the camellia petals. Bryce never used to care for the rain and previously he would have refused to go out. But now he insisted on going into Amalfi. Without any apparent discomfort he walked bareheaded in the storm while Claudine, wearing boots and raincoat, walked beside him feeling thoroughly soaked.

They walked as far as the cathedral then stopped at a fish restaurant where Bryce wanted to have lunch. It was a small, dim little place, with three or four tables covered with red-and-white-checkered cloths. The smell of fish pervaded the room. It smelled more like a fishing boat than a restaurant. The proprietor, a short, stocky man with a bristling black mustache, emerged from the back to take their order.

After Bryce had given their choices, Claudine shook the water off her jacket.

"This rain's a nuisance," she said, meaning it as a sort of joke. She was the one who usually insisted on walking in the rain and Bryce was the one who was always grumbling and calling the rain a nuisance.

Bryce looked at her as if suddenly recollecting himself.

"I'm sorry. Are you cold? I know you don't like the rain. I shouldn't have made you come on this walk."

Claudine looked at him closely to see if perhaps he was joking. But the look on his face made it obvious that he was sincere. Claudine was puzzled. How could Bryce have forgotten that she liked walking in the rain? It struck her as very odd. She recalled her earlier fears that Bryce's memory had been affected by the accident. The doctors had assured her it wasn't.

She began to think of all the differences in Bryce that she had noticed since the accident. There was his reaction to her selling the boutique. Before, he had argued with her incessantly about it and now he said that he thought she shouldn't have sold it. And then there was his affectionate use of endearments, he called her "my dear" and "my love" all the time now.

And then there was his surprise and horror the other night when she mentioned how they used to argue.

But all that *could* be due to just a change in attitude. Or perhaps an attempt to forget the unpleasant things that came before the accident. But how could he think she didn't like the rain?

Their food was brought to the table. It was a simple meal of fresh fish, wine and garlic bread. Claudine looked closely at Bryce as he ate. If he was having problems with his memory he was evidently trying to keep it hidden. Of course he would be worried about his job, worried that if they found out his memory was impaired they wouldn't let him work in such a delicate area of research. He wasn't going to admit to any form of amnesia, that was clear.

Claudine decided that she was going to have to watch him closely and see if she could determine for herself if there was anything wrong with his memory. That would be the only way she could help him.

"Is something wrong?" Bryce asked, noticing that she wasn't eating.

"No. I was just thinking. Do you remember the first time we went out for fish?"

"Of course I do," he replied, smiling. "I hope this rain clears up before we leave. One of the guests was telling me about some nearby ruins that would be fun to see."

Claudine listened to him, wondering if he was intentionally being evasive or if she was just being overcritical. If he did have amnesia it was only partial, and it was going to be very hard to determine without having him guess what she was doing.

THEIR LAST FEW DAYS at Amalfi were beautiful. The sun shone brilliantly every day and they took long walks together. Bryce had finished with the reports he had brought with him and so spent all his time with Claudine. Claudine had never felt closer to him.

One evening she recalled a night at the theater where they had laughed a lot but had ended up quarreling later.

"It's a shame that it didn't end as well as it began," she said.

"I don't remember how the play ended," he replied.

"No, the play had a happy ending. I'm sorry, I shouldn't have brought it up. It's ancient history."

Claudine covered it up as best she could, but it was apparent that he had no idea what she was talking about.

There was another time when they were talking about a friend of his named Charles, and Claudine couldn't remember his surname.

"What on earth is his last name?" she asked.

"Charles? You know just as well as I do."

"No, I don't. What is it?"

Bryce just gave a good-natured shrug and changed the subject.

Claudine was afraid of asking too many questions and putting him on his guard. Besides, she was enjoying herself too much. She had never had anyone treat her with as much loving kindness as Bryce was doing now.

Still, he kept his distance. The night that he had kissed her so passionately was evidently not going to be repeated. It was almost as if he had acted in spite of himself and was taking extra precautions to ensure that it didn't happen again.

Out of all the wonderful things they had seen and done in Amalfi, Claudine knew it was that kiss she would remember longest.

Chapter 9

Before moving to Autun, Bryce had some problems to sort out, and when they returned to Paris he went immediately to his office.

In the evening he was more nervous and irritable than he had been since he had left the clinic. And each day he seemed increasingly tired.

He would leave early in the morning, have lunch in the cafeteria and return late in the evening, exhausted, his features drawn and his face pale. Even so, each day he was going to a physiotherapist for exercises that he hoped would eventually restore the use of his right hand. Claudine could not persuade him to take things more slowly, and she hoped fervently that the effort wouldn't prove to be too much for him.

Their neighbors found Bryce distinctly odd, and one of them even complained to the superintendent because Bryce had passed him by without greeting him.

"It's not as if it's me whose face is changed," he grumbled.

The superintendent repeated the story to Bryce. Bryce kept silent in front of him but as soon as he had left he exploded.

"Does he really think I want to talk to those people? They stare at me like a monkey in a zoo. For a while I thought they were going to throw me peanuts."

"You shouldn't pay any attention to them."

"I'd just like to get out of Paris. At least I'll be left in peace in Autun."

This was yet another change in Bryce's character. Bryce had been difficult to live with but he had always been sociable. Now he not only avoided the neighbors but he refused to see any friends, as well. He claimed he was tired, which was true. But he wouldn't go out, nor would he have people in, not even William, who had been so close in the past.

Not wanting their apartment to remain empty while they were in Autun, Claudine was trying to sublet it. Sophie knew of an English couple who had to spend six months in Paris for business reasons. They would be moving to France in May, which left Claudine and Bryce enough time to find a place to live in Autun.

Claudine began to put their personal belongings in order: the clothes they wouldn't be taking, which were few, because the ones Bryce had taken to the tailor still weren't ready; the papers and knick-knacks and other little things that they were fond of. Among these was a porcelain statuette of a woman bathing that had belonged to Bryce's mother. Claudine tried to be very careful but she was so worried about damaging it that it slipped out of her hands and smashed on the tiles of the bathroom floor.

Claudine herself hadn't cared much for the piece but Bryce had always been attached to it. She tried to repair the damage but it was hopeless. She was horrified, certain that it would lead to an unpleasant scene, which would destroy their newfound harmony.

When Bryce came home and saw her face he knew something had happened.

"What's the matter? You look as if there's been a disaster."

"There has. I broke the porcelain statuette that you liked so much."

He laughed, apparently relieved. "You should be celebrating. That's one less ornament to dust."

His reaction was comforting, but Claudine was shocked.

"It was the one that belonged to your mother."

"It was only an ornament. Did you really think I'd be angry about something like that?"

Claudine had hardly recovered from her astonishment when the doorbell rang. It was Sophie, offering to come over the following afternoon and help prepare the apartment for the new tenants.

With commendable effort she avoided staring at Bryce, whom she hadn't seen since the accident.

"Hi, Bryce."

"Hello," he responded abruptly. Then, without even excusing himself, he walked out of the apartment.

"Did he leave because of me?" Sophie asked.

"No, it's not you. He's just been that way lately. He still feels uncomfortable around other people."

"Oh." Sophie looked at her for a moment, then smiled. "You're certainly right about his looks,

though. He is much better looking than he was
before."

"Thank goodness you didn't tell him that. He gets
terribly upset when people comment on his looks."

"Well, I guess I'd better be running along. I hope I
didn't cause you too much trouble."

"It's all right, Sophie. He's just very touchy about
visitors."

IT WAS AFTER NINE when Bryce returned and the dinner Claudine had cooked was cold. She sat quietly,
waiting to see what he would do.

"You could at least have told me you were expecting someone," he said angrily.

"I wasn't expecting her. And usually you're pleased
to see her."

"Usually!" he cried. "What's usual anymore? I've
told you again and again that I don't want to see
anybody. I just want to be left in peace. Why can't
you explain that to your friends and have them come
over some time when I'm not here?"

"She only wanted to help me organize the apartment. I thought it was kind of her."

"You've told her we're leaving? Do you have to tell
everyone what we're doing?"

"Don't be ridiculous, Bryce. How could I not tell
Sophie we were leaving? She's the one who found a
tenant for us."

Bryce suddenly looked anxious, as if he had committed a huge blunder.

"That's right. I'm sorry. I guess I must have just
lost my head. I've been so tense and tired lately."

Claudine watched him closely as he left the room.
She was positive that Bryce hadn't known that their

visitor was Sophie until Claudine had mentioned her name.

Claudine was becoming increasingly convinced that the accident had in some way affected Bryce's memory. There just didn't seem to be any other explanation for his strange behavior and evasive answers to questions.

She didn't know what to do. Both Bryce and the doctors insisted that there was nothing wrong with his memory. If there was, Bryce was trying very hard to hide the fact, and he would not like it very much if she were to expose him. But how else could he be helped? He would have to admit to the problem before anyone could help him.

But Claudine was hesitant to confront him with it. She was afraid that it would cause a breach in their relationship. And Claudine was so happy, happier than she had ever been. She loved Bryce with a deeper and more mature love than she had before and she was desperately afraid of having anything come between them. But what would her happiness be worth if Bryce was sick and needed help?

Before she did anything, Claudine wanted to be certain that Bryce's memory really was affected. She decided to call one of Bryce's close colleagues and see how Bryce was getting along at work. Surely if his memory was faulty it would show up quickly in the intense pace of his specialized job.

She called Gerald Ferreaux, the man who worked most closely with Bryce, and asked him if he noticed anything different in her husband.

"Physically he tires quickly, which isn't surprising. Initially I felt he was on his guard, but now I'm used to the changes and he seems more at ease."

"You don't have the impression that his memory's impaired?"

"His memory? Absolutely not! Obviously we made progress during his absence, but he's worked enormously hard and made up for the time he lost. Believe me, his memory is fantastic."

Claudine thanked him and hung up, feeling foolish. The doctors had been right all along. If there was something erratic in Bryce's behavior, the explanation didn't lie in a faulty memory. Claudine told herself that she would be extremely careful about becoming so suspicious again.

In mid-April Bryce left for Autun. Claudine would join him as soon as he found somewhere for them to live. In the meantime he would stay in the hotel.

The company had given him a new car. Claudine was very uneasy about the idea of him driving alone.

"I promise to be very careful," he vowed. "But if I don't try now, I might never be able to again. They say when you fall off a horse the first thing you should do is get back on."

"Have you ever ridden a horse?"

"Never."

As he kissed her goodbye his eyes were sad and she wondered if he was feeling the same thing she was. Often, before the accident, she had been quite happy to see him go away. But this time she felt strangely heavyhearted. She had become so much more attached to him in these past few weeks.

Claudine wanted to be ready to leave for Autun as soon as Bryce found a place to live so she busied herself completing the arrangements that had to be made in Paris. As soon as she had organized the things they wouldn't be taking in the basement, she

began to pack the suitcases. First, though, she had to
retrieve the clothes left with the tailor. When she
gave him the ticket, the tailor handed her only one
item, a tweed jacket. The suits, he said, had already
been collected. Claudine protested, but he showed
her his books, which recorded the date of delivery,
March 10, and the bill for the repairs. She was convinced there was some mistake, since on March 10
they had been in Italy. But she argued in vain; the
tailor insisted that Bryce's suits had been returned.

Four suits were a sizable loss, but when Claudine
telephoned Bryce and told him what had happened,
he scolded her for making a drama of a matter of
such little consequence. There was obviously some
confusion, he explained. Maybe the tailor had lost
the suits, but if that was the case his insurance would
reimburse them. He told her not to worry anymore
about it. He would look after it himself.

Since he had been in Autun he had looked at two
apartments, one was uncomfortable and the other
too small. But he had been given a lead on a house a
few miles out of town, which he was going to see.

Three days later Bryce called to announce that the
house had been so attractive he had taken an option
on it immediately. As soon as Claudine could see it
he would sign the papers and they could move in. He
said that if she had finished packing and was ready to
leave Paris, William, who had to go to Lyons in two
days, could pick her up on the way and would be
able to drop her off in Autun so that she wouldn't
have to move all the luggage by train. Claudine
didn't cherish the idea of driving such a long distance
with William, but as it seemed the easiest thing to do,
she agreed.

Claudine didn't know anything about Autun. To her it was just a name on the map. As they drove along, she asked William about the city and he told her that it had been one of the capitals of the Roman Empire and that the present city occupied only a fraction of the area of ancient Augustodunum, which had rivaled Rome in its splendor.

The town appeared on the distant horizon, nestling into the side of a hill; the old houses with their dark red slate roofs surrounded the tall cathedral, and farther down the hill, the white of the new buildings gleamed in the sunlight.

William dropped Claudine off at the Saint-Louis Hotel. The room Bryce had reserved for her was some distance from his own. Claudine bit her lip in disappointment. Evidently their recent separation had done nothing to allay his fears.

Claudine was in her room unpacking when Bryce arrived. Without thinking she kissed him. He returned her embrace warmly and Claudine was reminded with renewed force that she was passionately in love with him.

"It's only six o'clock," he said. "We have time to go and see our house."

"You've taken it before I've seen it?"

"No, but I'm sure you'll love it."

She did love it. They drove there through the streets of the old town, past the cathedral and down the valley again before climbing toward Couhard, where the house was located. It wasn't just a suburb of the town but was in fact a real village, built on the side of a hill covered with trees.

Bryce stopped the car in front of a wrought-iron gate. Through the bars of the gate, at the end of a flagstone path, Claudine saw a two-story building with a tiled roof. It was an old house, a little crooked, with slightly cracked walls, gray-painted shutters and a swallow's nest in the eaves trough.

"Let's take it!" Claudine said impulsively.

"Without even looking inside?" Bryce asked, laughing.

An enormous woman was waiting to show them around. Bryce introduced her.

"This is Maria, a neighbor. She has the keys.

The house was small. The ground floor consisted of one room and a kitchen, and the second floor had two bedrooms and a bathroom. However, the kitchen was well equipped and the bathroom had a full-size bathtub.

"There's a television, too," Maria explained. "And central heating. The furnace is in the cellar."

"Follow me," said Bryce, "you haven't seen the main attraction yet."

He opened the shutters in one of the bedrooms. Below the garden, a meadow planted with apple trees sloped down into the valley. Beyond the trees was a vast expanse of blue-tinged rugged mountains, and in the foothills the medieval city of Autun was encircled by ramparts, towers, fortified gate and a belt of trees. To the right was the vivid roof of a classical building and farther away, surrounded by green, swept a broad expanse of azure water.

"That's the military college," Bryce said, pointing. "And the lake so you can learn to sail. Lean out a little more."

Claudine leaned forward and saw a half-collapsed limestone structure.

"That's the Couhard stone, which was built by the

Romans. Don't ask me what it was used for because
no one knows, but it dates back to Vespasian and is
quite a famous local monument."

Claudine gazed out at the scenery, thinking how
easy it would be to be happy here.

"So," Bryce asked, "shall we take the house?"

"Of course! Let's move in this minute."

"You'll have to wait until tomorrow, since we
haven't any food yet," Bryce answered, laughing.

In the car he asked her again. "You're sure you
don't want to think about it?"

"Absolutely. I've fallen in love with it. It's in the
middle of the country but right by the town. And the
view is magnificent. It's much more beautiful than I
had ever hoped for."

"I agree. And we'll be able to take splendid walks
from here."

"Have you had time to walk yet?"

"I went to the Brissecou Falls. It's not as far from
Autun as it looks on the map and the doctor told me
walking would be good for me."

"Have you stopped your therapy?"

"No. I found a good masseur to help me and I
usually go there immediately after work. I'm glad we
both agree about the house."

Claudine was very happy about the house. But her
joy was tempered by one thought, which, try as she
might, she couldn't shake out of her mind: the house
had two bedrooms. And Bryce had gently but firmly
made it clear that they would both be occupied.

Chapter 10

The next day Claudine moved their luggage into their new home. The first thing she had to do was give the house a thorough cleaning. It hadn't been rented all winter and piles of dust and spiderwebs had taken over.

The more time she spent in the house the more she liked it. It was furnished in a simple, rustic fashion with brightly colored calico curtains. The windows let in a lot of sunlight, and after the dust had settled, Claudine could tell that it was going to be a very good comfortable place to live.

She had saved for the last the task of preparing the two bedrooms. Every time she thought about them she wanted to cry. In every other way Bryce was being such a kind and loving husband, more thoughtful and affectionate than he had ever been. And yet in this he refused to treat her as a wife. Claudine wasn't sure how long she could bear being closed off from him like this. She loved Bryce far more than she ever had and desperately wanted to be his wife and share

everything with him. But the doctor had warned her
not to rush him and she had seen from her own experience that it did no good to try.

Finally, she completed all the major tasks of moving in, including preparation of the two bedrooms,
and late in the afternoon she walked into Autun to do
some grocery shopping.

The road that led into town was quite steep but she
soon reached the tiny twisting streets leading to the
square, which in ancient times had been the marketplace and where now the town hall, the theater and
the military college, surrounded by its lavish gilded
railings, clustered. The marketplace itself had been
transformed into a parking lot and was full of cars. In
front of the school chapel Claudine discovered a
peaceful courtyard planted with trees. She would
have liked to explore further but she reminded herself
that she was not a tourist, she was a housewife.

She found the market and bought what she needed, which turned out to be so much that she had to
take a taxi back to Couhard.

When she arrived back at their little house with her
bags of groceries, she was overcome with a warm
feeling of home. She had never before felt so much
like a wife. Usually she had been so busy with her
boutique that the household chores had only
annoyed her and she would rush through them with
distaste. But now, as she put the food away in the
kitchen, she felt content. Everything she did—the
dusting, the scrubbing, the sweeping—gave her
satisfaction because she was doing it for Bryce.

She had decided to fix a special dinner in order to
celebrate their first night in their new home. A
woman at the market had given her a recipe for lamb

that she claimed had been a favorite recipe in the village since her great-grandmother's days. With the lamb, Claudine steamed some of the fresh local vegetables she had bought—mushrooms, carrots and cauliflower—and made a rich, savory cheese sauce to pour over them. She set the table with bright napkins and tall, creamy candles and even had time to go down in the garden and pick a bouquet of primroses before Bryce got home.

The fragrant aroma of the broiling lamb met him at the door and Claudine felt a rush of pleasure as she saw the appreciative look in his eyes when he saw all that she had done.

"You went to so much trouble. We could have eaten in town if you'd wanted."

"Not on our first evening here. I wanted to fix something special, something to make this feel like home."

"You must be tired," he said with gentle concern.

"Not really. But you look as if you are."

"I'm exhausted," he admitted with a deep sigh. "I guess I haven't got used to it yet."

"Sit down and let me pour you a Scotch."

"You didn't buy any vodka or gin, by chance?"

Claudine looked at him, surprised. "No. I got Scotch because that's what you've always liked. I'm sorry, I should have asked you first."

"Scotch will be fine," he said, but to Claudine, the tone of his voice made him sound as if he was taking medicine.

Bryce was silent while Claudine finished fixing dinner, too tired to make conversation. Claudine tried to fill the silence by cheerfully telling him about all the things she had done that day.

But when the food was set on the table and Bryce had tasted the succulent meat and perfectly cooked vegetables, he seemed to lose his fatigue.

"It's funny how quiet it is out here," Claudine said. "I keep getting the feeling of being somewhere at the end of the earth."

"It's the silence," he replied. "At first that's all you hear, but then you start noticing all sorts of noises. You'll hear the breeze through the trees, and the insects, and the birds at dawn. You'll get used to it. This area's so peaceful that you feel completely isolated, but in fact our nearest neighbor is only two hundred yards away. And we do have a telephone if there's any emergency."

"Oh, I'm not frightened. It's just different, that's all."

"Would you have preferred to live in the town?"

"No! Absolutely not. I love this house."

When dinner was over Bryce was extravagant with his compliments.

"I have never in my life had such a wonderful meal," he said. "I'm simply amazed that with all the cleaning you've done you found time to make such a delicious dinner."

Claudine smiled happily and felt that every bit of work had been well worth it if it made Bryce feel proud of her. But she was still slightly self-conscious about his compliments, and she tried to change the subject.

"Is your research progressing? How far are you now?"

He put his finger to his lips.

"Shh. It's top secret."

"But you needn't worry about me," Claudine

assured him. "Even if you explained exactly what you are doing I'm sure I wouldn't be capable of repeating it because I don't understand any of it."

"But the night has ears," Bryce said, only half-joking.

Later, buried under her blankets, Claudine listened to the strange country noises in the night and regretted having assured Bryce that she wasn't frightened. Perhaps if she had said she was terrified he would not have made her sleep alone. Claudine wondered what would happen if she were to go into his room and tell him she was afraid of sleeping alone. She knew that she shouldn't and she fought against the idea, but finally the impulse won out. She got quietly out of bed and walked noiselessly toward his room. Without knocking she turned the handle of the door. It was locked from the inside!

Angry with herself, she went back to her own bed. It made her feel foolish to think that Bryce had evidently expected her to try something like that and had prepared for the eventuality. All the happiness she had felt that day was whisked away like a dead leaf in the wind. As she fell asleep her heart was heavy.

CLAUDINE SLEPT LATE the next morning and by the time she awoke Bryce had already gone. On the kitchen table he had left her a note.

You were sleeping so soundly I didn't want to wake you. I'll see you this evening. Love, B.

Love? Claudine thought about all the different meanings that word could have. She thought of all the overpowering feelings in herself that she used that word to describe and wondered what meaning the word had for Bryce.

She was just finishing her coffee when there was a knock on the door. A little old gentleman with white hair and matching mustache smiled pleasantly at her when she opened the door.

"I hope you'll excuse this early-morning visit," he said, bowing slightly. "I just wanted to be sure there was nothing you needed. I'm Henry Dupin, your closest neighbor, wine merchant...and entirely at your service."

Claudine smiled and invited him in.

"Would you like a cup of coffee?"

"No, thank you. I've had breakfast already. Do you like the house?"

"Very much."

"Ah, that's good. You see, I'm also your landlord. When the previous owner decided to sell, I bought it, thinking that it would be nice to be able to choose my neighbors."

Claudine thought that he must be very rich to be able to afford such extravagances.

"Are you from this area?" she asked as they sat down in the living room.

"No, I'm from Normandy originally, but I've lived in Couhard for two years. I was looking for somewhere I could retire to when the time came, but I didn't want to move too far away from Lyons, where my business is, and I can't bear the south. You look baffled by my choice, but you'll understand when you get to know the region better."

"How did you happen to choose this area? Did you come here just by chance?"

"I stayed in Autun when I was a boy. It's lost its former charm, of course, but it's still attractive. I have some books about the area that I can lend you if you like."

He went on to describe his adopted city as he had fallen in love with it fifty years earlier, with its old police headquarters miles away from the main roads, its sleepy streets—its existence almost forgotten by the outside world. After the war it had been spoiled by industrial development and had become the regional capital. Dupin disliked everything new in the city. He found the new buildings too impersonal, and there seemed to be more cars than livestock on the square on market day. All the elms that used to shelter the square had disappeared, and the man-made tiles that had replaced the beautiful old varnished tiles on the roof of the cathedral were abominable, and so on.

"They could have done better than turn the market square into a parking lot," he said. "Go there at six o'clock and you'll find yourself surrounded by harassed drivers looking for parking meters, immigrants, laborers and housewives talking to one another in all sorts of foreign languages. In the old days everything in Autun had its origin in the past. And you could just walk around the quiet streets and dream about all the history that had taken place there. But now there's nothing left except the area around the cathedral where the old hotels are, and the law courts. And even there there are always dozens of tourist buses, full of foreigners and noisy old folk on those ridiculous golden-age tours."

Claudine found the old Mr. Dupin amusing and quite pleasant to be with. He wanted to show her his house and invited her for lunch, but she refused and instead made a date to have a cup of tea with him on the following day.

After saying goodbye, Claudine wondered whether when Bryce had chosen this isolated spot he had intended that they should make friends so quickly.

Claudine spent the remainder of the day finishing putting their belongings away. This chore, which at first had seemed endless, was over sooner than she had expected. Still full of energy, Claudine was wondering what to do next when she had an idea. Bryce had talked quite a bit about the new laboratories where he was working and he had even mentioned once that she should come and see them. She had never been to Bryce's place of work, even before the accident, and she thought that it might be fun to pay him a surprise visit.

Flushed with excitement and feeling rather nervous at what suddenly seemed an adventure, Claudine quickly bathed and dressed in a smart green pantsuit. A soft cream-colored wool turtleneck set off her dark eyes and fair skin and she brushed her chestnut hair till it shone.

She called a taxi to take her to the suburb where the company had built its new facilities. The laboratories were unimposing, consisting of just two low buildings surrounded by a garden. Claudine located Bryce's office and was just about to knock when the door was suddenly opened from the inside by one of the most beautiful women Claudine had ever seen.

She was tall and slender and her long blond hair was loosely wrapped on top of her head. Her slanted light green eyes and high, prominent cheekbones lent her face a coolly exotic air. Although the woman was probably a few years her junior, Claudine felt suddenly awkward and schoolgirlish under the other's steady gaze.

"May I help you?"

"I was looking for Bryce...Mr. Chevalier...my husband...." Claudine wasn't sure what to say.

"Oh! Mrs. Chevalier, I'm very glad to meet you." The young lady smiled warmly. "I'm Frances, your husband's new secretary. Won't you come in? Bryce will be back shortly. He didn't tell me he was expecting you."

"He wasn't," Claudine said, and laughed nervously.

Bryce's office was neat and functional looking, with large bay windows that looked out over the garden. The secretary left and Claudine sat down in a chair to wait for her husband.

A few minutes later Bryce came in and saw her. His startled look made Claudine wonder with a sinking heart if her little surprise visit hadn't been a big mistake.

"Claudine!"

"I'm sorry, Bryce, I didn't mean to bother you. I just thought I'd drop by and see how you were...."

"And I'm glad you did," Bryce said, overcoming his surprise and kissing her lightly. "I wanted to show you around the new place and this would be a perfect time to do it."

With great relief Claudine let Bryce take her on a tour of the lab. Bryce stopped for a long time by the coordinator, who was assembling the results of the experiments, explaining to Claudine that this was an expensive investment, but indispensable.

As they were leaving the lab, Bryce suggested that he cancel his appointment with the masseur and they could go out to dinner. "There's a restaurant I've heard about called the Old Windmill. It's on the river, very close to the Roman gate."

Claudine gladly accepted the invitation but wondered about his guilty air. He seemed to be trying to hide something.

Bryce caught her looking at him suspiciously and suddenly burst out laughing.

"All right, I guess I'm no good at keeping secrets. I was going to surprise you but you may as well have it now."

Bryce led a mystified Claudine outside to the parking lot and handed her a key.

"There you go. Yours is the yellow Fiat."

"Mine?" Claudine exclaimed.

"I managed to get a very good deal on it. It's small, but I think it will be very useful for you." Bryce's deprecatory tone couldn't allay the gaiety in his eyes.

Claudine was ecstatic and thanked him again and again until Bryce had finally had enough and threatened to take it back if she thanked him again.

The restaurant was beautiful, and in high spirits Claudine chatted happily throughout the entire meal. Bryce listened with an indulgent smile, now and then asking her questions.

"And what have you done today?" he asked. "Or did you spend the whole morning planning this surprise visit."

"Not at all. As a matter of fact I've been so busy I had to turn down an invitation to lunch."

"I didn't realize you were so sociable," he said, lifting his eyebrows.

Claudine laughed. "It was just our landlord, Mr. Dupin. I've agreed to have tea with him tomorrow."

"Dupin? Oh, yes, he is our neighbor, isn't he?"

"He seems very pleasant."

"I met him for only a moment after I signed the lease. He seemed like a harmless old fossil to me."

"He's very interesting," Claudine insisted. "And I think it takes a lot of spirit to move into a town where you have no connections."

"When you see his house you'll know why," Bryce laughed.

Worried about money and the amount that Bryce must have spent on the car, Claudine asked him if he had ever straightened things out with the tailor about his suits.

"Yes, that's all settled. The tailor admitted he lost them and is going to send me a check," Bryce replied, and then changed the subject.

The evening went so well and Claudine felt so close to Bryce that, late that night when they returned home, she couldn't bear the thought of having to sleep alone. Against her own better judgment she threw herself into his arms and when he tried to draw back from her close embrace she protested.

"Don't push me away, Bryce, I'm your wife!"

"I thought you understood that we have to wait." His tone was severe.

"No! I don't understand! The scars don't matter to me. All I know is that I love you."

With more force than Claudine would have thought him capable of, Bryce grabbed her by the shoulders and held her stiffly at arm's length. His jaw was clenched, and the expression in his eyes was both fierce and pleading. When he spoke, his low, constricted voice gave evidence of a conflict within.

"If you truly love me then you will allow me to wait until I've worked this thing out for myself. You must know how important it is for me to be alone until I've got rid of the nightmare that haunts me day and night. If you truly love me you won't ask me to give you something that I can't give you without causing great harm to myself. What kind of love would it be if it demands no consideration for the other person?"

With that he turned on his heel and strode into his bedroom. The sound of the key turning in the lock was final and irrevocable.

Chapter 11

All night Claudine lay awake listening to the sounds of the darkness, trying to calm the storm of emotions that raged inside her. She didn't cry. She just lay there, silently listening. It was not until she heard the birds on the hillside signaling the approach of dawn that she was able to fall asleep.

Claudine woke late but did not feel at all rested. In the cold morning sunlight all her confused emotions had narrowed down to one solitary fear. She was dreadfully afraid that her impassioned outburst of the night before had caused an irreparable break in her relationship with Bryce. She was horrified at the thought that she had let herself go so far and had perhaps ruined the greatest happiness she had ever known.

In the kitchen she found a note from Bryce.

Dearest Claudine, please forgive me. Believe me, I love you. B.

The brief note allayed the worst of her fears, but at five o'clock, when she was to have tea with Mr. Dupin, Claudine was still agitated. She composed herself as best as she could and walked over to her neighbor's house.

The beautiful eighteenth-century house was hidden behind high walls and surrounded by a park. It had two floors with high ceilings and mansard windows set into an irregular roof. A double staircase with marble balustrades led to the front door. Virginia creeper grew over the lintel and between each pair of shutters on the ground floor, its light green blending with the autumn colors of the tiles.

The door opened and Mr. Dupin came out to greet her.

"Now I know why you decided to come to Autun," Claudine said, looking admiringly at the house.

"Isn't it beautiful? The wall around the park hides the view unfortunately. I'm afraid our ancestors attached less value to scenery than we do. Did you notice the facade? It's just like the Millery Hotel, which is the most beautiful building in Autun."

"I'm afraid that I haven't been around the town yet," Claudine said almost apologetically.

"You've got plenty of time to see it. Come inside."

The room he led her into had an incredible mixture of furniture. There were Regency desks, Louis XV chairs, worn leather sofas, Chinese tables, Art Deco tables, and strewn on top of them all were piles of books, papers and magazines.

"Please ignore the mess. I have a woman who comes to do my housekeeping four times a week, but even that isn't enough. The furniture is a bit of a crazy mixture. I can't afford to buy the style worthy of my folly. And for an old bachelor like me to buy an old house like this that needs so many repairs certainly is a folly!"

"You don't regret it!"

"Not for a moment."

He showed her through a string of five rooms on the ground floor, and after climbing the wide steps of a curved staircase, they looked at three more rooms tucked away in the roof. After the tour he took her back to the drawing room, where they were to have their tea.

"Those," he said, pointing to a pile of books, "are for you. In them you will find everything you would want to know about your town."

Over tea, Mr. Dupin began to describe the cathedral to Claudine with a wealth of detail and humorous anecdotes, making interesting what otherwise would have sounded like a boring lecture. From there he went on to the traditional belief that the old gates of Rome had been used in the construction of the medieval porch, then to the legend of Saint Ladre, and finally mentioning Ingres's satisfaction with his painting of *The Martyrdom of Saint Symphorien*. Mr. Dupin took such delight in the stories he was relating and had such an ability to pick out only the most interesting and significant facts that Claudine found it quite pleasurable to listen to him.

"Here I am going on like an old chatterbox," he said after a while. "Why don't you tell me something about yourself?"

Hesitantly at first, Claudine began telling him a little about her past. She told him about her family back in the States, her dream of starting a boutique and selling her own designs in the fashion capital of the world, and her modest success in making the dream come true. Soon she was so comfortable talking to him that she was freely telling him about Bryce and her marriage and the accident that had almost killed him. Mr. Dupin's deft questions led her into talking about her reaction to Bryce's surgery and how much the whole thing had changed him.

Suddenly Claudine realized how much she had revealed about her personal life and she stopped, feeling somewhat embarrassed by her own lack of discretion. Mr. Dupin quickly took over and led the conversation back to other matters. A short while later Claudine bid the old gentleman goodbye, thanking him for the pleasant afternoon and promising to visit again soon.

When Claudine returned home and was beginning to prepare dinner, Bryce called from work and said that he would be home late. The tone of his voice was kind and he made no mention of the scene of the night before.

Tired from her lack of sleep during the night, Claudine decided to lie down for a short rest. She stretched across her bed and soon fell into a deep sleep.

The click of the front door closing. Slowly Claudine began to struggle out of her dreams. On the stairs the sound of footsteps. Claudine turned over onto her back, trying to shake the grip of sleep. Now the sound of someone walking down the hall toward her room. Claudine opened her eyes.

In the darkness a narrow band of light from the hall sliced through the slowly opening door. Claudine sat bolt upright, every nerve instantly alert. Barely breathing, with blood pounding in her ears, she stared with distended eyes at the growing oblong of light.

Suddenly it was blotted out by the silhouette of a strange man.

Claudine screamed.

Light flooded the room and Claudine saw that the stranger was Bryce. She sobbed as he rushed forward.

"Claudine! What's wrong? Are you all right?"

Claudine nodded. It took a moment for her to find her voice.

"You gave me such a fright! I guess I must have been half-asleep."

Bryce put his arms around her still trembling shoulders.

"I'm sorry, my love. I didn't know you were sleeping."

Claudine relaxed against him, letting him hold her and calm her down. Then suddenly she sat up.

"My goodness, what time is it? You haven't had dinner yet!"

"It's nine o'clock," he said, helping her to her feet. "I got home later than I expected. You gave me quite a start, as well, you know. When I came in the house was dark and you weren't anywhere around. I was worried that something might have happened. And then when you screamed like that, I didn't know what to think."

They went down to the kitchen together. Claudine turned on all the lights, trying hard not to dwell on the residue of fear that still caused her to tremble inwardly. She cut several slices of the cold leftover lamb and put them on a plate with some of the mellow, local cheese. She got out some bread and wine and set everything on the kitchen table.

They were both hungry and the simple meal tasted good.

"I don't know," Bryce said thoughtfully after they had eaten. "Maybe we should have found a place a little closer to town."

"I'm not scared, Bryce. And we do have a telephone if there's ever an emergency."

"But you should at least keep the doors locked."

"Bryce! We're out in the country now, there's no reason to keep ourselves all locked up." Claudine was surprised at his concern.

"Still, I wish you'd be more careful. It can't hurt."

That night Claudine watched Bryce as he carefully locked all the doors and windows on the ground floor. Although she had just had quite a fright, she couldn't help but be puzzled by his sudden caution.

Clutching the covers tightly around her, Claudine told herself that it was silly to be frightened. But try as she might, she couldn't shake the fear that hounded her. Silly as it was, she couldn't get over the feeling she had had when she had seen his silhouette in the doorway. She tried to tell herself that she had still been half-asleep, but she knew that wasn't true. Her eyes had been wide open. There was really no way around it: when she had seen the silhouette in the darkness she had instinctively reacted to it as to a stranger's. And the feeling had been so strong, so certain, that even after the lights had been turned on, Bryce had seemed to her to be an unfamiliar man clumsily trying to play the role of her husband.

Claudine told herself that the whole idea was just too ridiculous, and putting the pillow over her head, she forced herself to go to sleep.

The next day the thought was still in the back of her mind. She felt uneasy sitting across from Bryce as he drank his coffee before going to work. Silly as it seemed, she kept thinking of all the things that were different about him, all the things he seemed to have forgotten, all his evasive answers and his attitude of secrecy.

But how could Bryce be someone other than himself? She told herself that the idea was perverse, that it was like something out of a science-fiction movie. Nonetheless, over the days that followed, the idea persisted.

Part of her problem, she knew, was that she was alone so much. Bryce left early in the morning and didn't come home until dinnertime, and sometimes he even had to work later than that. The only other person that Claudine had any contact with was old Mr. Dupin, who would come over every day and chat for a bit, talking mostly about the history of the province.

When the weather was fine she would walk through the nearby forest, where there was a beech grove with a stream running through it and a small waterfall. On other days she would park her car in the market square and wander through the old streets around the cathedral and the law courts, or down past the boutiques on the rue aux Cordiers.

One morning, after passing a restless night worrying over the enigma of Bryce, Claudine decided to call the tailor in Paris and check the story of what had happened to the suits. When she mentioned the compensation paid by the insurance company, the tailor interrupted. There was obviously some mistake, he said, as there had been no question of loss and there had been no compensation. The suits had been returned, against a receipt, to a messenger sent by her husband.

This time Claudine was determined to ask Bryce for an explanation.

"Yes, I did lie," he admitted without embarrassment. "You were worrying so much about my expenses that I didn't dare tell you I'd lost the receipt. Someone obviously found it and used it to claim the suits. It was just bad luck, and since it was my fault, there was no question of claiming insurance. Don't worry, it wasn't that much money."

He seemed to have answers for everything, but his reply was so slick that Claudine only half believed him.

The more she tried not to think about them the more discrepancies she saw between the Bryce she had known before the accident and the Bryce she knew now. Finally, to put an end to the silly thought once and for all, Claudine decided that she would have to find some way to determine for certain that Bryce was still the same person that he said he was.

By no means did she want Bryce to find out what was on her mind. That would make her feel too ridiculous and would probably offend him, as well. So she had to find some way of making sure without Bryce's knowing about it.

She had one idea but it didn't seem too feasible. Bryce had a small birthmark on the left side of his chest. Claudine remembered that the nurse at Mountain Spring had said that Bryce's chest had sustained little damage. The trouble was, with Bryce's phobia about keeping his body completely covered, there was no way she could look at his chest without his being aware of it.

Claudine tried again to put the whole thing out of her mind. After all, she had known Bryce for only a year before the accident, and it was very likely that the changes in his behavior, which seemed to her so odd, were really quite characteristic of him. And besides, why would someone want to impersonate her husband? The whole thing was ridiculous.

Bryce was acting more and more troubled. He was tense and distracted, but whenever Claudine asked him if something was wrong he would just say that he was working too hard.

A few days after the night he had frightened her so badly, Bryce came home with a pistol. Though she said that she didn't want to touch it, Bryce insisted on showing her how to use it. He put it in the drawer of the lamp table in the living room and told her that if anyone ever did threaten her, she shouldn't hesitate to use it.

THE FOLLOWING DAY Claudine was just setting down her bags of groceries on the kitchen table when the phone rang. Shrugging out of her jacket, she breathlessly picked up the receiver. The voice at the other end was unfamiliar, but warm.

It was Dominique, Bryce's sister. She had just arrived in Paris and suggested, if it was convenient, that she drive down and see them that very evening.

Claudine was overjoyed. Here was the perfect way to put to rest her silly fears about Bryce. His sister would certainly know her own brother.

In order that Bryce wouldn't try to avoid the meeting with Dominique, Claudine decided not to tell Bryce about the phone call. She prepared a meal, but didn't set the table, and with stubborn hope changed the sheets on her bed. Dominique would have to sleep somewhere and it was only natural for Claudine to offer her bed.

Bryce arrived home a little before seven. Dominique was due to arrive at any moment.

"You haven't set the table," he said. "Would you like to eat out?"

"No, it's all ready. I'll serve it in a few minutes."

Every time she heard a car Claudine tensed. Eventually Bryce noticed.

"Is there anything wrong?" he asked.

Before Claudine could reply, a car slowed down and stopped in front of the house.

"Are you expecting someone?" Bryce asked, walking over to the window.

A Renault was parked in front of the gate and a large woman dressed in tailored tweeds got out.

"Dominique!" Bryce groaned. His face went deathly pale. Then, without warning, he ran out the front door to meet this sister at the gate.

From the window Claudine saw Dominique hesitate a moment, then embrace her brother. They stood by the gate talking for a few minutes, and then Bryce led her into the house.

"Why didn't you tell me Dominique was coming?" Bryce chided her, only half-joking.

"I wanted it to be a surprise," Claudine replied, and embraced her sister-in-law, whom she had never met.

Bryce and Dominique talked excitedly while Claudine set the table. Bryce was asking her endless questions about her family and kids and what she had been doing for the last few years. Claudine couldn't help smiling to herself. Bryce and Dominique had recognized each other immediately.

The dinner went splendidly but Claudine was disappointed to find that Dominique wasn't planning to spend the night. She had an aunt in Saint-Rémy that she was going to see, and she said that she would prefer to get there that night.

Claudine managed to get a moment alone with Dominique before she left.

"So what do you think of Bryce?" she asked nervously.

"I think that they did a marvelous job on his face," Dominique replied.

"But what about the way he acts? Does he seem much different to you?"

"Different?" Dominique eyed Claudine skeptically. "No, not at all. He seems just the same as always."

Completely relieved, Claudine let Bryce walk his sister out to her car while she cleared the table and started the dishes. Bryce talked to Dominique for a while outside before she finally left.

Bryce came back in and handed Claudine a slip of paper with Dominique's address on it.

"Don't lose that, it may come in handy," he said, going over to pour himself a drink.

Claudine noticed that his hand was shaking as he raised the glass to his lips. She went over and hugged him.

"What's wrong? Was it so bad? It seemed to go quite nicely."

"Yes, it went all right," Bryce said, looking at her sternly. "But I don't at all appreciate being surprised like that and I would be quite happy if you never did it again. It could have been....it could have been a disaster."

Chapter 12

A week later they received another visit, this one unexpected to both of them. William had a week's vacation and had decided to spend it in Autun seeing the countryside. He didn't want to trouble them too much and insisted on staying at a hotel in town, but he was counting on them to show him around.

"In fact he's counting on you," Bryce said. "He knows I haven't time to take any days off at the moment."

"Does his visit bother you?"

"A little. But at least you'll have some company."

The next day was Sunday, and when William came over, Claudine set out a delicious meal of chicken in a creamy sauce and a variety of subtly seasoned vegetables.

"I didn't know you were a cordon bleu cook!" he commented, surprised.

"Neither did I. I'm on the point of becoming the perfect lady of the manor."

"In other words, you're bored."

"Bored? Not at all. I have too much to do, what with cooking, looking after the house and gardening."

"You work a garden?" William said, truly surprised. "The Parisian in the fields?"

The tone of their conversation seemed to be annoying Bryce.

"I tried to get Claudine out doing something," he interrupted. "But she says that she's more content staying at home."

After lunch they drove to Lake Settons. The weather was miserable. A cold mist hung over the mountains, gorse bushes carpeted the hillside in dull gold and herds of white cows huddled damply together behind the thick hedges. As they strode through the dripping undergrowth they startled frightened birds into flight.

"This isn't a very joyful place, this countryside of yours," William commented dryly.

"You're seeing it on a bad day," Bryce protested.

At Settons the rain began to fall, as fine as Breton lace, blotting out the horizon completely.

"It's a shame," Bryce said. "When the weather's fine there are always lots of sailboats on the lake and it's very picturesque."

"Does sailing appeal to you?" William asked Claudine.

"Only if Bryce would come, too. But not alone."

"And won't he take you?"

"I'm not allowed any sports," Bryce interjected brusquely.

"I'm sorry," William said. "I was forgetting your accident."

The rain began to fall harder, shrouding the mountains in uniform grayness. The walk was turning out poorly, so they decided to return home.

"What on earth do you do in the provinces when it rains?" William asked condescendingly when they got back to the house.

Bryce frowned, but before he had time to retort, Claudine replied.

"I haven't even had time to think about that yet."

'Why? Has the weather always been fine?"

'No. It's because I'm happy. It's amazing how much time being happy takes."

This statement was followed by a silence. Looking perplexed, William watched as Bryce came over and put his arm around her shoulders.

"Thank you, my love," he said, looking into Claudine's eyes.

When Bryce returned from driving William home, he seemed preoccupied.

"It something wrong?" Claudine asked.

"William irritates me with his snide remarks on country life. And he thinks he's funny. I wish that he hadn't come."

"But you used to enjoy his company so much."

Bryce began to put his papers in order.

"What's upset you, Bryce? Surely not one rainy day?"

"No. It's William's being here. Before, with you, I was beginning to forget..." He stopped. "Don't pay any attention to my bad humor. I'm overloaded with work at the moment. That's all."

Claudine found the next few days tiring. Her distaste for William grew the more she was around him. He had a scornful and belittling attitude toward her, the same type of attitude in fact that Bryce used to have before the accident. She found his humor rather crude, and his constant inquiries into her relationship with Bryce made her feel ill at ease.

But he was a guest, and since he had no interest in seeing the mountains in the region, she conscientiously escorted him around Morvan, Beuvray, Pierre-qui-Vive, Arnay-le-Duc and Semur-en-Auxois.

In the evenings they would have dinner with Bryce, either at a restaurant or at home. Bryce was irritable, serious and preoccupied. He obviously found William's presence a burden.

William was to stay a full week and leave on Sunday. After he had gone back to the hotel on Friday, Claudine went to sit in the garden for a while. The day had been hot and the evening was cool and refreshing.

Bryce came and joined her, sitting on the grass near her chair.

"Only two days to go," he sighed.

"Does he bore you that much? You used to be so entertained by him."

"I don't have anything to say to him anymore. You're right, he does bore me."

He leaned his head against Claudine's knee and she slowly ran her fingers through his hair.

"Why are you so sad?" she asked him. "Aren't you happy with me?"

"You? If only I could take you away from all this mess, then I'd be happy. If only we could be left alone to start a new life together."

He seemed to have some deep trouble that he was keeping locked within. Certainly he couldn't be this

upset because of William. Claudine could not understand what it could be. They had a nice house, his job
seemed to be going well, even if it did require a lot of
work—what could be causing him this anguish?

For a long time they sat together, Claudine trying
to think of some way to ease his troubles but unable
to do so. Her heart felt near to breaking to see him so
disturbed without being able to help.

Suddenly Bryce stood up and, sounding angry
with himself, he bid Claudine good-night. Hurt and
puzzled by his strange change of moods, Claudine
sat for a while longer in the garden, wondering
what she had to do to become Bryce's wife again,
in the full sense of the word. There was some secret
that Bryce wasn't sharing with her, a secret that was
keeping her from attaining that perfect joy she longed
for.

The night before he was to depart, William had offered to take them out to dine at Carre-les-Tombes.
But first, Bryce had to stop off at the laboratory.

"Come in with me for a second, William. I've got
something you might be interested in," Bryce said.

Alone in the car, Claudine turned on the radio to
see if she could find out what the weather was going
to be like. She was only half listening when the
newscaster said something that made her sit up
straight.

"Our news staff has today reported further
developments in the story of the Savoy surgeon who
was arrested earlier this month. It has been confirmed that Dr. Leroux and his assistant may be held
in custody for several months pending an investiga-
tion into an alleged conspiracy to abet the escape
of criminals. The doctor, who specializes in plas-

tic surgery, is under suspicion for having assisted known criminals by performing surgery to alter their facial structures and change their fingerprints. A spokesman for the doctor's defense said, however, that the charges are based on mere rumor and that there is no evidence—"

Claudine quickly switched the radio off as Bryce and William returned to the car.

"Are you ill?" Bryce asked, looking at her pale face. "You look dreadful."

"I have a slight headache, that's all. I'll be all right."

Claudine stared out the window, trying to fend off the feelings of confusion and nausea that threatened to overwhelm her. She tried to make sense out of the story she'd just heard.

Just because Dr. Leroux had been accused of something didn't mean it was true. And besides, even if it was true it didn't mean that it had anything to do with Bryce. Leroux must handle hundreds of patients a year. They couldn't all be criminals.

When they reached the restaurant, Claudine was so distraught that she didn't want to try to sit through dinner making polite conversation.

"I really don't feel very well. Why don't you two go ahead without me?"

Bryce looked at her with concern.

"If you aren't feeling well, we'll go home," he said.

"No, I don't want to ruin your dinner. You two just go ahead. I'll lie down here in the car. I'll be all right; it's just a headache."

Bryce protested but Claudine's insistence won out and the two men went in to dinner, leaving her alone with her thoughts.

She tried to tell herself that the whole thing was just a crazy coincidence, but her earlier fears rose up so strongly that she couldn't be satisfied with such a simple explanation. All the things that had seemed so different about Bryce since the accident, all his lapses of memory, all the odd feelings she had had that he was really someone else—it was too much for her. She knew that she wouldn't be able to sleep another night in the same house without finding out one way or the other. She had to know if the man she had come to love so strongly over the past few months was her husband or a complete stranger.

But how was she going to find out? She couldn't just ask him. Suddenly her hopes surged as she remembered Dominique's visit. Bryce had recognized his sister, and she him. Didn't that prove that he really was Bryce?

For a minute Claudine was happy, thinking that she knew for certain that the man she was living with had to be Bryce. Then her hopes fell. How naive she was. The whole visit could easily have been arranged. The woman could have been anyone—Claudine wouldn't have known. She had never met Bryce's sister before. Claudine was again besieged by doubt.

She was certain that if she could get Bryce to take off his shirt she would be able to recognize him by the birthmark on his chest. But how could she get him to take off his shirt unless she absolutely insisted? And under those circumstances, if it turned out he was her husband after all, what would the effect on him be? With all his phobias about his body and his abhorrence of people looking at him, if Claudine forced him to take off his shirt, it could very well mean the end of their happy relationship.

Having evidently rushed through their meal, Bryce and William returned to the car. Since Bryce had to stop at the lab, he suggested that they drop him off there and he would take a taxi and meet them at home. Claudine didn't protest.

Still not feeling well, she let William drive. After they had dropped Bryce off at the lab and were passing through town, Claudine asked William to stop at a drugstore so that she could get some medicine. While waiting in line at the counter she quickly glanced through the newspapers. It didn't take long to find what she was looking for.

The two-column article said that although Dr. Leroux had just recently been arrested, the police had been suspicious of him for a long time. The paper even detailed the method that the doctor was accused of using to operate on criminals without notice. The "patient" would arrive by ambulance, either on a Sunday or on a public holiday, when Leroux was on duty alone. The patient would always be admitted as a road accident, operated on immediately and isolated in intensive care. By the time he was admitted into the general ward he was just another patient.

William came into the drugstore to see what was taking her so long and Claudine handed him the paper, pointing to the article. Puzzled, William slowly read the story. When he had finally finished he looked at Claudine, his eyebrows raised quizzically.

"I'm afraid I don't understand—" he began, but Claudine excitedly interrupted him, her new fears overriding her usual caution and her dislike of William.

"Can't you see? Leroux was Bryce's doctor and everything that it says is exactly what happened to Bryce—the road accident, admitted on a Sunday, isolated in intensive care—"

"Calm down, Claudine. Take it easy now." Nervously glancing around, William led her outside. When they were seated in the car he tried to soothe her.

"Even if this Leroux character is guilty of what he's accused of, what has that to do with Bryce? If Leroux was dealing with criminals who were trying to escape detection, he would be providing them with new identities. What good would it do the criminal to have to impersonate a man who has a wife and family? That would just guarantee his getting caught."

What William said made sense. It wouldn't be practical to try to have the criminals impersonate other people. They would be given new, fabricated identities. Claudine knew it didn't make any sense, but it was too much to just be a coincidence.

"I know it sounds crazy," she said. "But you see, I've had the feeling for a while now that Bryce isn't really Bryce."

Claudine went on to tell William all the things that had struck her as odd about Bryce. When she had finished he just shook his head.

"It still sounds crazy to me."

"I know," Claudine agreed. "But I can't stand the doubt anymore. I've got to find out for certain whether or not Bryce is really my husband."

"And how do you propose to do that?"

"I think that if I can just get him to take off his shirt I'll be able to tell."

"Well, good luck." William started the car.

"But you've got to help me!"

"How? You want me to hold him down while you rip off his shirt?"

"How can you possibly joke about this?" Claudine demanded.

"Because I don't believe a word of it. It's all just your imagination. You're losing your mind! You'll gain nothing by making Bryce furious."

"Does that mean you won't help me?"

"No. Since you insist on going through with this, let's go."

Bryce was not at home when they arrived. What if he had heard about the accusations lodged against Leroux and wasn't coming back? Claudine was too upset to know what to think.

"I'm letting you go through with this," William said, "because I'm certain of the outcome. If I weren't sure, I would call the police. You are amusing yourself by making yourself frightened. You don't even seem to have considered the fact that a criminal impersonating someone else, like the wolf in 'Little Red Riding Hood,' could be dangerous."

Claudine realized that William was not taking her seriously. "I hope I'm wrong," she said. "I hope so passionately. But if I don't find out the truth tonight I'll end up in an asylum."

The sound of an engine silenced them. Bryce walked in, calm and assured.

"How are you feeling?" he asked as soon as he saw Claudine.

She handed him the newspaper article.

"What is this?" he asked after quickly glancing through the article.

"Bryce, take your shirt off, please," Claudine said in a trembling voice.

"Take my shirt off! What's the matter with you?' Bryce glanced at William, who only shrugged.

"Come on, Bryce," Claudine persisted.

"Why? Because of that article? That's ridiculous!"

"Don't stand there talking about it," William intervened in a resigned but authoritative voice. "Just do as she asks and get it over with."

As if completely disgusted by their little domestic drama, William walked over and leaned casually against the front door.

Bryce glared at him, hesitating for a moment. Then, turning his back on William, he walked over and stood in front of Claudine. Staring straight into her eyes he began unbuttoning his shirt.

He hadn't even reached the bottom button when Claudine laughed nervously. She had seen enough.

"I'm sorry, Bryce. I don't know what's wrong with me. I feel so silly."

"Satisfied?" William asked.

"I made a fool of myself. I hope both of you can forgive me."

William evidently judged it best to leave them alone, and, her knees still weak, Claudine walked him out to the gate and bid him a smiling goodbye. She stayed by the road for as long as his car was in sight, and then she walked back into the house.

Bryce hadn't moved from where she had left him. Claudine closed the door and then walked over to the lamp table.

Bryce realized too late what she was doing and he

was only halfway across the room when Claudine turned around.

She was pointing the pistol straight at his head.

Chapter 13

Bryce stood still, looking at her with a sort of amused surprise in his eyes.

"Who are you?" Claudine asked, her voice almost breaking.

He looked at her, intrigued.

"If you knew I wasn't Bryce, why did you lie in front of William?"

He was right, she had lied. Almost without thinking about it. Instinctively she had covered up for the man she was now pointing a gun at. She had done her best to get him out of a compromising, perhaps fatal situation. But she wasn't about to admit to him that she had done it because, despite all the agonizing truths she had just stumbled upon, she was in love with him.

"You killed my husband," Claudine stated tremulously, still holding the gun on him.

A look of incredulity came over his face.

"You really think I did that and you haven't called the police?" he replied with what sounded like wonder in his voice.

His reactions were disconcerting Claudine and it was hard for her to keep her voice from shaking. But she had to stay calm if she was to ever know the truth.

"I have to know if you killed my husband." She looked closely into the eyes that she had come to love, knowing that he would not be able to lie to her without her knowing it.

"I swear that I didn't kill your husband."

Claudine stared at him until she was certain that he was telling the truth. She felt an odd sort of relief.

"You didn't kill him, but he is dead?"

He nodded.

Claudine set down the gun, which she knew now that she had never intended to use, and shakily sank to the couch.

"My dear Claudine," he said, and his voice had the same tone it had had these many months since the accident. "I would have done anything to spare you such terrible news."

Claudine wondered if in fact she really wasn't going insane.

"What's happened to my husband? Did friends of yours kill him?"

"No. In fact we have no evidence that he was murdered, though personally I'm convinced that he was. I was told that he died accidentally."

Claudine closed her eyes and clenched her hands. Her head was spinning in circles, and she thought for a moment that she might faint.

"Lie down, Claudine. Let me get you some cognac."

This pretense of kindness destroyed her calm completely.

"I've had enough of playacting," she screamed. "Bryce is dead and you've been living here pretending to be him for months. Why? What's the purpose of doing this to me?"

It was too much for her to handle. She must have fainted because when she opened her eyes, Bryce was kneeling in front of her holding out a glass.

"Drink up now. You'll feel better."

Her arms felt heavy as she slowly took the drink. Feeling as if she were moving in slow motion, Claudine gulped the cognac. It burned in her throat and brought her back to life.

She looked down at the man kneeling before her. There was still that look of anxious kindness in his eyes, which over these past few months she had become accustomed to. Yet now there seemed to be a sort of curious wonder, as well. She told him to stand up.

"What's the point in carrying on this role playing now that I know you aren't Bryce?"

"Obviously I haven't been doing a very good job of it anyway, since you weren't deceived."

"You didn't prepare your ground well enough. You gave yourself away in the first note you gave me at Mountain Spring. Bryce would never have written a note like that."

"I didn't write you that note. I would have preferred telling you the truth long ago but it would have put you in unnecessary danger." He frowned, hesitating slightly. "And to be quite frank, I didn't want to be the one to have to tell you about Bryce's death. I know how much his death affected me, and I hadn't seen him in years. I would rather not have been the one to cause you the pain of knowing, though of course you would have to know eventually."

"You knew Bryce?" Claudine's head began to swim again. "Who are you? Are you on the run from the police?"

"From the police? No, nothing like that."

"You didn't answer me. Who are you?"

He looked down at her as if weighing all the possible replies, as if considering a new scheme. Then, with a sort of shrug, he replied in a flat voice, "I'm Christopher Chevalier. Bryce's brother."

The alcohol, which had now gone to her head, gave Claudine a strange feeling of detachment. She leaned forward and studied him attentively.

Undeniably there was a resemblance to Bryce. There were certain gestures and mannerisms. And his voice on the telephone often sounded like Bryce's old voice. And it would explain the great number of childhood memories and also explain how Dominique recognized him. If that had, in fact, been Dominique.

Claudine stared at the man who was now smiling wryly under her intense scrutiny. He could very easily be Bryce's brother. Then again, he could just as easily be playing another game with her.

She looked directly into his eyes, which openly met her gaze. She felt an odd anxiety in the pit of her stomach and realized that she could not bear to doubt the sincerity that she saw in his eyes.

"Christopher? But why? How could you? How could you work with your brother's killers?"

Claudine stood up and began pacing. He took hold of her wrists and forced her to sit back down.

"I want you to listen to me very carefully,

Claudine. I'm not sure how much time we'll have now, and this might be my only chance to explain everything to you. I was not involved in Bryce's death and I'm not working with the people who killed him. I'm working for Interpol. I'm in counter-espionage."

"That doesn't make any sense. Bryce couldn't have had anything to do with espionage."

"That's because in your mind spies are only interested in military secrets. But in this day and age industrial espionage is much more important."

"You mean his research?"

Christopher sat down and took a deep breath. 'The person most responsible for everything that has happened is Bryce himself. Did he ever talk to you about his research?"

"He always thought I was too stupid to understand it. All I know about it is what I've heard from you."

"Basically, the research is on the development of a synthetic fuel that can be mixed with gas at about fifty percent. Not only would this automatically double a country's fuel supply, but it is also lighter and has many possible applications as a rocket fuel. It could conceivably give land-based missiles a striking range never before dreamed of."

"I still don't understand where Bryce comes in."

"Just listen now. I explained that the principal activity of spies these days is industrial espionage: for every one man working in the military there are ten in industry. Everyone is mixed up in it—big companies, as you might expect, but also small, rival companies, where more or less amateurs sell the information they collect. In the long run there is so much money involved for the companies that engage in this kind of activity that they will stop at nothing. You can't imagine the methods some of them use, or how long they will wait. We have arrested Soviet agents who had lived for more than twenty years under a false identity, with a wife and children, simply in the hope of receiving some useful information.

"The way you discover where to look for information is very simple. All you have to do is read and compare carefully the specialist journals in an industry, and the company reports and financial statements. In this case it was a loan taken out by Bryce's company to build its new laboratories that gave the clue, because the government put pressure on the banks to ensure the best terms. Someone therefore considered the affair to be worth following up."

"A foreign government?"

"According to the information we've obtained, probably not. Apparently Bryce was contacted by someone who said he was a messenger from an organization that was interested in certain kinds of information. Initially the information asked for was harmless, and the remuneration was given so discreetly that he let himself be drawn in. The majority of agents are recruited in this way. One small compromise, and then blackmail. When Bryce realized what he had fallen into, he managed to regain control of the situation.

"Through one of his friends, a magistrate, he got in touch with Inspector Vidame in our department. Vidame had heard of a number of similar cases and was convinced that neither the C.I.A. nor the K.G.B. was involved. Everything seemed to point to an independent middleman who, after obtaining the information, would be prepared to sell to the highest

bidder. Bryce had only two contacts and he didn't
know who controlled them. The department asked
him to continue supplying unimportant information
in the hope that he would be able to get through to
the heads of the organization.

"For a short time he acted as a double agent, but
then something went wrong. They may have noticed
the uselessness of the information that he was passing
on. At any rate, they decided to activate their plan to
infiltrate one of their own men in the laboratory."

"By killing Bryce so you could take his place?"

He sighed impatiently. "You still don't understand.
What the organization needed was a chemist, a specialist. They had one in their hands, a man brilliant
in his field but whose weakness for gambling had put
him at their mercy. They had used him before. He
was the one who had been verifying the information
supplied by Bryce. He was hopelessly in debt, com-
promised by his earlier dealings with them and
desperate enough to do anything. He was nearly the
same height and build as Bryce, and the same age.
Leroux could do the rest."

"How do you know all this?"

"From this chemist. His name is Durand."

"And he told you that the organization had murdered Bryce so that he could replace him?"

"No. According to him, Bryce was killed accident-
ly. He was drowned when swimming in a lake with a
young German who was a member of the organization. The organization had the idea about the
substitution only after he was dead. I don't believe
that version myself. You can't improvise a scheme of
this magnitude. It has to be prepared in minute detail
and therefore requires time.

"But however it happened, the fact was that Bryce was dead, and the organization faked the car crash and had Durand taken to Mountain Spring, where Leroux went to work on him. For the first two months it was Durand you saw in the isolation room, covered with bandages, and he was the one who wrote those first messages to you. He would still be impersonating Bryce if Vidame hadn't decided to intervene."

Claudine had stopped listening. She was thinking about all the anguished weeks she had spent at the bedside of a bandage-covered figure who had been a complete stranger.

Christopher noticed her distraction.

"What are you thinking about, Claudine?"

"About all that time I was with Bryce, and how I suffered with him and admired his courage. And he was dead."

"Claudine, I sympathize with what you must be feeling right now. I know it's hard, but you're going to have to pay attention. You might as well get the whole story straight now, because I don't know how much time there'll be for this later."

His curt tone hurt her, but it made her realize that there was more at stake here than her own emotions.

"Even if his face was changed, how did they expect to be able to get away with it?"

"They gave him precise information about the minutest details of Bryce's life. Durand knew all his habits and his eccentricities. Any unavoidable contradictions would be put down to the accident. Naturally it would have been easier to fake amnesia, but an amnesiac can't be expected to take part in delicate research projects. He knew, and the or-

ganization knew, that the risks were enormous. But
the stakes were high and for a gambler like him it was
tempting. Moreover, if he had refused, he would
have been killed."

"Did the chemist tell you that?"

"No. He persuaded himself that he was working
for people incapable of killing, but the extent of his
fear tends to contradict him on this point. Apart
from the money I believe it was fear that made him
agree to have surgery on his face and his body
scarred so badly. He wasn't without courage,
however, because although he didn't have to suffer
the terrible injuries described by Leroux, he had to
undergo considerable surgery. On the other hand, he
was being hunted by the police and it was definitely
in his own interests to change his face and his fingerprints."

"Did he end up looking like Bryce?"

"Not really. But he looked completely different
from before. His own mother wouldn't have recognized him. Leroux changed his vocal cords to give
him a new voice and provided tinted contact lenses,
like actors sometimes use, in order to match Bryce's
eyes."

"But surely he didn't hope to deceive me forever.
Eventually I would have seen his body and then I
would have known."

"That's what all the phobias and psychiatrists were
for. They had all been worked out by the organization for the chemist's use. They foresaw the danger
you presented to their plan, and although your
presence was much to their benefit, if you had shown
the least bit of doubt they would simply have killed
you, as well."

Claudine shivered. She was getting a better idea of the extent of the intrigue. She wondered if she would have been duped by the chemist as easily as she had been by Christopher.

"How did you get mixed up in all this?" she asked, trying to overcome the fear that was beginning to rise up again.

"Really just by chance, although Vidame likes to claim it was through his genius. The organization committed two errors: they didn't know Bryce was in touch with Interpol, and they didn't know that Leroux's activities had already come to the attention of the police. Several months previously the police had installed an observer, disguised as a nurse, at Mountain Spring. For some time Bryce hadn't been feeling safe and had told Vidame so. Therefore, when Vidame learned that he had been in an accident and had been taken to Mountain Spring under suspicious circumstances, and that Leroux had operated on him with the sole assistance of his nurse, Vidame was immediately suspicious. His observer at Mountain Spring, who was on the police force, was responsible for verifying whether the wounded man in the isolation room was, in fact, the victim of intensive burns."

"How did Vidame get the idea of the second substitution? It sounds so complex."

"Not to him. He's been involved in many major cases like this. When the nurse had determined that the patient in the isolaton room wasn't suffering from burns, that in fact, at the time, the only thing that had been done to him was a face lift, Vidame had her take the man's fingerprints, which hadn't yet been altered. We were than able to determine just who he was.

"By this time the police had enough evidence to arrest Durand, Leroux, Jeannette, the German and Bryce's contacts with the organization. But Vidame wanted to get the top people."

"Couldn't Durand and the others tell him?"

"That's assuming they knew them. But Vidame knew through Bryce that the organization was as tightly controlled as a professional spy network, with each agent in contact with only two or three others. It would have been impossible to work up the chain. It was the organization's audacious plan that gave Vidame the idea for his yet more spectacular one to replace the chemist with one of his own men. He didn't have too much time at his disposal and he had to find someone who could replace Bryce without too many changes. I had worked with Vidame once long ago, and so, when his research showed that I was Bryce's brother, I was his natural choice."

The story was almost too fantastic to believe. Claudine would have laughed, if it wasn't for her certainty that the man sitting next to her was not her husband and yet had fooled her for months. Fooled her even to the point where she had fallen in love with him.

Chapter 14

Her thoughts and feelings in a whirl, Claudine demanded incredulously, "But are you a chemist?"

"That was my first objection to Vidame's plan," Christopher explained. "He told me, though, that I had time to become one. You see, in order for the substitution to succeed, I had to stay in the hospital for several months, or even longer if the new laboratories weren't ready by the spring. This gave him time to get me ready. I didn't have to know enough to pass any exams, just enough about a limited field to convince people that there was no reason for them to question my qualifications. They said that they would help me and they did. I had lessons every day, even in my first hospital."

"Your first hopsital?"

"In order to take Durand's place I had to have similar scars to his. They made only superficial marks on me, except for my nose. I'd broken it twice and so I allowed myself the luxury of corrective surgery at the expense of the department. I also had

to learn to wear contact lenses, but mine are color-
less. Bryce and I have our father's eyes. However,
this didn't stop me studying. I had a professor at
Mountain Spring, too."

"You mean you replaced Durand at Mountain
Spring? When? Didn't Leroux notice?"

"He wasn't there by then. Vidame was kept informed on a daily basis and learned that Durand
wouldn't come out of isolation until after Leroux had
gone. Leroux was barely on the plane to the Caribbean before I was in Durand's bed."

"What happened to Durand?"

"With his consent, the police have put him in a top
security prison. He knows his only chance of getting
out of this is if the organization is exposed. If not, he
won't escape alive."

"But even with his cooperation, how can you hope
to succeed? The organization knew Durand."

"The operations made him unrecognizable."

"Someone at Mountain Spring might have seen
him after his operation."

"Other than Jeannette and Leroux, no one saw
him. None of the members of the organization would
have dared to risk going there."

"But when Leroux or his nurse got back to France,
couldn't they have given you away?"

"They were both arrested the minute they set foot
in this country."

"And hasn't Leroux's arrest alerted the organization?"

"He is being taken to court on some old charges
that have nothing to do with the organization, and
accordingly to my contact, the organization has
broken all association with him."

Claudine carefully tried to put all this information in order. It seemed immensely important to get everything straight once and for all to clear up the confused delusion she had been living for the past months.

"But Dominique must have recognized you as Christopher. Or wasn't that Dominique?"

"Yes, that was Dominique all right. But when I ran down to meet her at the gate I warned her not to say anything. I couldn't explain it all to her, but she knows me and I've been in tight places in the past. She also knows about my work with Interpol and she must have guessed that I was in a dangerous situation. I'm very lucky she's as quick as she is and had the presence of mind not to give me away."

"You certainly took enormous risks."

"So did the chemist."

"Yes, but he did so because he was frightened and stupid. What was your reason?"

The question visibly bothered him and he sat frowning for a moment before answering.

"When we were kids together I treated Bryce rather poorly. He very much needed my support, the type of love and support that one expects from a brother. And when I could have helped him I turned my back on him. He never forgave me for the way I treated him, and afterward, when I saw how badly I had hurt him, I felt pretty ashamed. So I guess I agreed to do this as much for atonement as to avenge his cold-blooded murder."

"You told me that you have no proof he was murdered."

"We don't. And perhaps never will. We searched the lake for his body but weren't able to find it.

However, I believe a crime did take place, not just because their plans demanded a lot of preparation, but because the accident happened at the exact moment when the company's experiments were interrupted by the building of the new labs. It all fits together too well."

"So you are risking your life to atone for some childhood callousness? If you're discovered, won't the organization kill you?"

Christopher just shrugged. "I'm on my guard. And besides, it won't be the first time I've been in such a tight spot."

Claudine looked at him closely. She wanted to believe him, but how could she be certain? He could just as easily be working for the organization as against it. But what could she do? If she went to the police, they would probably just think she was crazy. She had no proof of anything. And besides, if Christopher was working for the organization he would probably get rid of her in some manner if he suspected that she didn't believe his story.

Her emotions were too confusing to sort out. All she knew was that she'd been tricked into loving the man sitting across from her. And even though she now knew she'd been tricked, it didn't seem to matter.

"It's absolutely necessary that you believe me," Christopher went on. "Personally I wanted to tell you from the start. I thought that it would be much easier if you knew and then we could have convinced you to take a trip or something where you would have been safely out of the way. But Vidame thought that if we could keep you from suspecting anything it would be safer for me to have you here. Just as the organization reasoned that their plans were safer if you were kept around. For who would think of doubting a man's identity if his own wife didn't? But now that you know, we'll have to get you away to someplace safe."

"But if I leave now, won't that give you away to the organization?"

"It might, but I'll just have to chance it."

"Wouldn't it be better if I stayed and pretended to believe you were Bryce?"

Christopher looked at her with admiration. Then he shook his head.

"It's too risky. If the organization gets even the least bit suspicious that you don't think I'm Bryce, they would do away with you immediately. And after that scene this evening I think they're going to be highly suspicious."

Claudine didn't understand his last statement.

"How could this evening give it away? The only person who saw what happened was William and—"

Claudine stopped, her eyes widening.

Christopher looked at her wryly. He nodded.

"William is my contact with the organization."

"William!" Claudine's face registered shocked disbelief. "He was Bryce's oldest and closest friend."

"Think about it," Christopher said. "Who was the only person close enough to Bryce to persuade him to involve himself in such a venture? William. Who was the only person who could provide so much detailed information about Bryce's character and past to the organization? Who else but Bryce's dear friend William."

"But to be in league with his best friend's

murderers? I find that hard to believe, even of William."

"William doesn't believe that Bryce was murdered. He believes in the story of the accident. He's been working for the organization for years and, like the chemist, doesn't want to admit to himself that he's working with a bunch of killers. Industrial espionage doesn't usually go to such lengths."

"Then he thinks you're Durand?"

"Hopefully."

"Then he probably knows that I was lying earlier."

"Not necessarily. He has no way of being certain. He has mentioned, though, that he thinks you might be suspicious of me. I've done my best to convince him otherwise, but after this evening, I don't know. The important thing right now is to get you to a safe place."

"But if William is already suspicious, won't he be certain if I leave right after that last scene?"

"I'll just have to deal with that later. But if you stay around here there's too great a chance of your getting hurt."

"It's a little late to start worrying about my safety, isn't it?" Claudine retorted, annoyed at being treated like an obstacle.

Christopher raised his eyebrows. "Well, what do you suggest?"

Claudine stood up and began pacing back and forth. She stopped in front of Christopher. "I think that I should stay at least long enough to convince them that I still believe you're Bryce. If they see that you're trying to protect me, they'll immediately become suspicious that you aren't Durand. They know that Durand would have no reason to protect me."

Claudine didn't know why she was talking this way or what she really wanted. She knew that she should hate Christopher for deceiving her as he had these past months. But instead, here she was insisting on risking her own life so that he wouldn't be left alone in such a dangerous situation. She looked up to see Christopher looking at her with frank admiration.

"Are you really willing to try that? Do you really want to stay and try to convince them that you think I'm Bryce?" Christopher studied her intently.

Claudine hesitated, uncertain of what he was asking.

"I don't know," she finally confessed. "What do you think I should do?"

Christopher smiled gently and stood up.

"I think that you should get some sleep. You're in no condition to be making such decisions right now."

Claudine nodded in agreement, then suddenly found herself crying uncontrollably. Christopher reached out to put his hand on her shoulder, but then hesitated. Without thinking, Claudine threw her arms around him and sobbed against his chest.

After a long while she calmed down enough for him to lead her upstairs to her room. She fell quickly into a troubled sleep.

CLAUDINE WOKE THE NEXT MORNING feeling tired. She lay in bed staring at the ceiling, trying to put everything in some kind of order. The pain she felt over Bryce's death felt like an old pain, as if she had known about it for months. Along with the pain was fear, fear of forces that she had no control over, forces that were so much stronger than she was that they could will her without flinching. And underneath the pain and fear was her confusion over her feelings for Christopher.

Before, when she had believed that he was Bryce, to love him had seemed so natural, so good. But now what was she supposed to feel? Before it had made her happy to love him. Now she didn't want to. It seemed wrong. And hopeless. But she couldn't allow herself to think of the future. Not yet at least.

A light knock on her door interrupted her thoughts.

"Come in."

Christopher opened the door and came in carrying a tray with coffee, orange juice and toast.

"I thought that you might like some breakfast, my love."

The endearment startled Claudine. At first she thought that he was deliberately trying to hurt her, but then she realized that, although the knowledge of what was going on was new to her, he had been living with it for months. She began to appreciate how difficult his task had been.

He set the tray down on the bed and then went over and opened the shutters, letting in a flood of morning sunlight. He came back and sat down on the edge of the bed, eyeing her closely.

"How are you feeling this morning?" he asked with sincerity.

"I don't know, Christopher—" she began, but was quickly cut off by his hand covering her mouth. His face had the look of frustration that a parent has with a child who doesn't know any better.

"You *must* believe me, Claudine," he whispered. "This is a very serious affair. You must remember always to call me Bryce."

"I'm sorry," she murmured contritely when he had uncovered her mouth.

They sat for a moment in silence. Then they heard someone in the garden. Christopher got up and went over to the window.

"Excuse me," old Mr. Dupin called out. "I rang the bell, but you must not have heard."

Claudine put on her housecoat and joined Christopher at the window. He put his arm around her shoulder and drew her close. Entwined like this they presented the ideal image of a young couple in love. Dupin looked up at them, smiling.

"It's for you to excuse us," Christopher answered. "We kept you waiting. I'll be right down."

"No need! My morning visit had only one purpose, which was to assure myself that you, my dear young lady, were well. But since I can see that you are, I can go on my way in peace."

"It was kind of you to worry about me," Claudine replied with forced cheerfulness. "Can I invite you to lunch tomorrow?"

"Why don't you come to my house instead? I wouldn't like to impose any extra work on you."

"No work at all. It would be a pleasure. I insist that you come."

"Under those conditions, I accept. I'll see you tomorrow, then."

He turned and walked back in the direction of his house. Christopher watched him go with a thoughtful expression.

"You must be very careful what you say to him, Claudine," he said earnestly.

"Surely you don't think there's anything dangerous about old Mr. Dupin, do you?"

"Nothing except that he's a nosy old chatterbox, and that in a small town like this a little news goes a long way."

Christopher grasped her hand tightly.

"This is a very dangerous game we're playing, my love. You will have to be on your guard every moment. When William stops by this morning to say goodbye, you'll have to do absolutely everything you can to convince him that things are still all right between us. It's vital!"

WHEN CLAUDINE ANSWERED THE DOOR, William looked at her intently. "So?" he inquired. "Are you feeling better?"

"I can't understand why I behaved so stupidly yesterday! If Bryce hadn't been so angry I would have laughed about it. I completely lost my head, I think. It must have been hearing about Leroux's being arrested that did it. And I've probably read too many detective stories." She laughed lightly.

"You aren't still doubtful, then?"

"Bryce has given me absolute proof of his identity," Claudine assured William. He still looked perplexed.

"What's the matter?" she asked him.

"Nothing, really," he answered slowly. "I'm sorry you imposed such a humiliating scene on Bryce. He could have done without it."

"He's forgiven me."

"Then who am I to prolong discussion of the issue."

Claudine was pouring coffee when Christopher

came downstairs. William's short visit passed without incident. Claudine acted as naturally and cheerfully as she could, giving no hint of the strain she was undergoing. Christopher was much more skillful and seemed to be completely at ease. However, they were both equally relieved when William finally left.

Christopher complimented Claudine on how well she had handled herself. She only wished that she could be sure that William had been convinced.

Claudine found that it was easier to keep up appearances when there was someone else there. That night at dinner she felt awkward and nervous. Christopher tried to get her to talk about Bryce and their marriage, but Claudine was reluctant to dredge up all the old disagreements and bitter arguments.

Instead, she got Christopher to talk about his past. She found out that he had had a varied and exciting life, full of adventures and close calls. She couldn't help but wonder if all this wasn't just another adventure to him.

Chapter 15

Mr. Dupin came to lunch the following day. The topic of his lively discourse rarely varied: Autun, its history, its people, its charm. Claudine had practically become an expert on the area just from listening so much to his entertaining conversation.

At one point, Dupin stopped and became serious.

"Is everything all right, my dear? You don't look well."

"Don't I?" Claudine said lightly. "I guess I'm tired. Bryce had to work late and I don't sleep well when he's out of the house."

"Are you sure there's nothing wrong?" the old man persisted. "You know, if you need help of any kind, I would be more than happy to oblige, even if it's just lending a sympathetic ear."

Claudine desperately wanted to unburden herself to the kindly old man. She needed to talk to someone who would sympathize with her. But she was conscious of Christopher's warning and did not give in to the temptation. Instead, she changed the subject by asking Mr. Dupin about the origins of the Couhard stone. He quickly launched into a speech that lasted throughout the remainder of his visit.

The next day Christopher came home early from work to report that he had to go to Paris. William had called him and asked him to come. It was urgent.

"I don't like it," Christopher confessed, fastening his case. "But I'll find out what he wants before I get worried about it. In any case, I'll be back late the day after tomorrow."

As SHE CLOSED THE DOWNSTAIRS DOORS and shutters that night Claudine couldn't help noticing how easy it would be to break into the house.

Nervous at having to spend the night alone, she had trouble falling asleep. And it was late at night when the sound of someone moving through the garden woke her.

Claudine lay motionless, stiff with fear and not daring to breathe, listening to the sound. There was the rustle of leaves, then silence.

Finally she forced herself to get out of bed, and, her heart pounding with fear, she tiptoed over to the bedroom door and locked it. Then, taking care not to make the floorboards creak, she crept across to the window. Peering through a crack in the shutters she stared down into the darkness. There was no moon and all she could see was the dark mass of apple trees. Nothing moved. Perhaps in her nervousness she had been mistaken. She waited.

Then, from among the other shadows, a dark figure emerged. Slowly and carefully it approached the house, then walked around it, out of Claudine's line of vision.

Her first thought was to call for help, but the telephone was on the first floor and she was too frightened to leave her room. The gun that Christopher had bought for her protection was downstairs, as well. Now Claudine understood what he had been worried about. The organization they were dealing with had already killed once and had nothing to lose by killing again.

Claudine pushed a chest of drawers against the door and crouched behind this barricade, listening for a long time for any suspicious sounds. Nothing broke the stillness of the night except, from time to time, the soft hooting of an owl. Still she sat, tense and waiting. It wasn't until she could see the gray sky of dawn from between the shutters that she lay down again and finally slept.

In the morning she put the chest of drawers back in place. By this time she had decided that she couldn't spend another night alone in the house, and since Christopher would not return until late the following day, she would get a room in the hotel in town.

Claudine also decided that the best way to discourage another visit would be to make the incident known. She smiled wryly at the thought that for once the small-town gossip was going to be an aid. She told the butcher and the baker and made a point of visiting Mr. Dupin before going into Autun.

Her news of the prowler seemed to amuse him.

"It must have been a tramp looking for somewhere to sleep the night, or someone wanting a few logs from your woodshed. We don't get burglars around this area. It was probably just being alone in the house for the first time that scared you." He smiled, obviously skeptical. "Take my advice and go to

Echarmeaux. You're too nervous and the mountain air will do you good."

His suggestion appealed to Claudine. The idea of going on an excursion and getting away from everything was very attractive. But before she could leave she had to go into Autun to reserve a room for the night. She went to get the car, then realized that Christopher had borrowed it a few days earlier and had forgotten to give her back the keys. So much for her trip to Echarmeaux.

It was a fine day, however, so Claudine packed a few things in an overnight bag and walked down to the Saint-Louis Hotel. After lunch she went to a movie, then bought two detective stories and went back to the hotel. But the books and the movie provided only a temporary distraction, and her mind continually went back to her ever present fears.

In spite of them she slept soundly and woke the next morning refreshed. She took a taxi back to Couhard, and as she alighted from the vehicle she was startled to see a man running down the path toward her.

It was Christopher.

"Where were you?" he demanded.

Claudine was shocked at how haggard he looked. "I stayed the night at the Saint-Louis Hotel. What's the matter?"

"I came back from Paris early and found the house empty and no word of explanation. I didn't know what had happened."

"I'm sorry. If I'd thought that you might be home this early I would have left a note."

They walked back up into the house and Claudine told him about the prowler. Christopher's face became tense.

"I like this less and less. William's questions in Paris worried me. He's sure you don't believe I'm Bryce, and I don't think I managed to convince him differently."

"Does he suspect that you aren't Durand?"

"No, thank God. It hasn't entered his head that a double switch could have been pulled."

"Then how does he explain the fact that I lied?"

"I'm not certain, but I think that he believes that you and I have come to some kind of agreement between ourselves to double-cross the organization. He didn't say so in so many words but I sensed that implication. But if the organization suspects that you know I'm not Bryce, they may be tempted to kill you. I'm going to take a close look around the house."

"You think someone might be hiding there?"

"Not someone, something."

Despite a meticulous search, Christopher found nothing unexpected. He was about to leave for the laboratory when it occurred to him to ask Claudine why she hadn't taken the car into Autun.

"You had the keys with you," she explained.

Christopher looked at the car thoughtfully.

"Claudine, I would like you to go back into the house while I check over the car."

Realizing that Christopher thought that the car might be wired to explode, Claudine refused to leave him, but finally agreed to stand back while he examined it.

There was no bomb, but Christopher did discover that the brake cables had been tampered with.

"You could easily have had an accident."

"Wouldn't I have noticed it as soon as I started?"

"Not likely. You could have gone ten or fifteen miles before anything happened. Then all you'd need to do would be to drive fast, or over the mountain roads, and you'd have lost control of the car completely."

Claudine shivered to think of how close she had come to being killed. If she had taken that little excursion to Echarmeaux yesterday she would probably right now be lying dead at the bottom of some ravine.

"Do you think we should tell the police?" she asked.

"Out of the question. It would be better to keep this to ourselves. Luckily I can repair this damage myself."

Christopher mended the cables and assured her that the car was now safe, but Claudine was not in any mood to go driving. She spent the day in Couhard, trying to keep her mind and hands busy with little chores around the house. She was in the garden pruning the rosebushes when Christopher returned at six o'clock.

"I'm glad you're here," he said. "I have to spend the night at the lab and I've come to pick up the things I'll need."

"Are you sleeping there?"

"Yes. I'm on guard duty. I'll explain to you later."

"Are you going to take a suitcase?" Claudine asked, following him inside.

"It's not worth it. Claudine. . . ." He stopped.

Claudine looked at him and was surprised by the anxiety she   his face He seemed like a man fighting against himself, trying to control some urge that he thought was wrong.

"Claudine, we are in a very serious position, you and I. If I don't come back, you mustn't wait for me. Leave as soon as possible. And go as far away as possible. Promise me you will do that."

"But what's going to happen? And I thought that it would be better for me to stay and try to convince them that I still think you're Bryce."

"Things have developed more rapidly than I thought. It looks as if the organization suspects us, and if that's the case, there's no telling what they'll try."

"I'm no more likely to get hurt than you are," Claudine reasoned, wondering what it was that Christopher was trying to say.

"Listen," he replied almost gruffly, "I just want you out of the way where I won't have to worry about you every minute. Now be a good girl and do as I say.

CLAUDINE WAS UPSET and nervous the rest of that night. Christopher's attitude troubled her and she regretted letting him leave without demanding more information about what he was doing. In the morning dark clouds piled up on the horizon and the air was heavy and oppressive. Christopher still hadn't telephoned.

Feeling abandoned and helpless, Claudine paced back and forth in the living room like a caged tiger, trying to think of an excuse to call the laboratory. At eleven o'clock the telephone rang. It was Christopher.

"Claudine? Is everything all right? No nocturnal visitors?"

"No. When are you coming home?"

"I don't know yet. I'll call you. I love you."

The tone of his last words suggested that he wasn't alone. Otherwise there was no need to keep up the pretense of a loving husband, she reasoned with a heavy heart.

In the afternoon, Claudine went down to Couhard to do a few errands. As she came out of the grocery store, she ran into Mr. Dupin.

"Is your husband away?" he asked. "I didn't see his car pass by my house this morning."

Provincial curiosity is legendary. Claudine couldn't help picturing Mr. Dupin watching eagerly from behind his gates, trying to figure out all that was going on.

"He had to stay at the lab last night," she replied. Heavy drops of rain were beginning to fall and she took advantage of them to cut the conversation short and hurry home.

As Claudine came up the path to the house she saw a stranger waiting by the door, a tall thin man with very fair hair and intense, light blue eyes.

Claudine stopped abruptly. She fought down the feeling of panic that urged her to turn around and run away. She thought of the prowler and how the brake cables had been tampered with and all of Christopher's warnings. The stranger by this time had seen her and was openly watching her. Finally she decided that any approach this open couldn't be too threatening, and she walked up to within a few yards of the man then stopped again, eyeing him carefully.

"Mrs. Chevalier, may I talk to you for a few moments?"

"What about?" Claudine asked cautiously. Despite the rain she didn't move any closer to the house.

"It's about your husband."

Claudine examined him closely. He was wearing brown flannel slacks and a worn leather jacket. He looked anxious and quite friendly. Nonetheless, she had learned enough at least to know that she couldn't assess people simply by how they looked. And she wasn't prepared to trust any strangers.

"I hope I'm not creating too bad an impression," the man continued humorously noticing her scrutiny. "Chevalier has talked to you about me, I believe. My name is Vidame."

Claudine continued looking at him skeptically. She found it hard to believe that this casual young man was Inspector Vidame. She had formed a different picture of the head of Interpol's department of counterespionage.

"Don't be alarmed," he went on. "I have proof of my identity. But please, could we move inside?"

Claudine hesitated a moment longer but decided, with the help of the rain, that she might as well trust him enough to invite him in.

"Where's Chevalier?" he asked once they were inside.

"At the laboratory."

"I've just come from there. He isn't there."

Claudine was still on her guard. "Well, that's where he told me he was. If he isn't there, I don't know where he is."

"In other words, you don't want to tell me." He sighed. "Here." He held out his identity card for her to see.

Claudine glanced at the card and shrugged.

"I still don't know where he is. He told me he was spending the night at the laboratory.

"My ID isn't good enough? Listen, I can repeat to you everything Chevalier has told you if it would help."

He went on to recount, in detail, everything Claudine knew already. Point by point, his story confirmed the one Christopher had told her.

"Now do you believe me?" Vidame asked when he had finished.

Claudine nodded.

"Then tell me where I can find Chevalier."

"He told me he was going to the laboratory."

"Well, he's not there now. He left yesterday at noon and hasn't been back."

"But he just telephoned me," Claudine said, beginning to get worried.

"What did he say? How did he sound?"

"He didn't say much, but he sounded all right."

"He must have called from somewhere other than the lab. He was supposed to get in touch with me yesterday evening but he didn't. Since I hadn't heard from him I went to the laboratory, where they say they haven't seen him since yesterday."

Claudine would have been more anxious if he hadn't called. She was convinced that he must have left the laboratory of his own accord.

"He didn't say anything that might give any clue as to where he was going?" the inspector insisted. "I'm beginning to wonder if he hasn't done something foolish."

"What do you mean?"

"At this point I don't know whether he's working for us or against us."

"Why would he change sides?"

"I don't know. All I do know is that he's disappeared without telling me. It's got me worried. If he has double-crossed us then we'll lose track of the organization. On the other hand, if he's gone to play a solo hand, the results won't be any better."

"What do you mean by that?"

"Chevalier doesn't much like operating by the book. He does things his own way and he doesn't care for people telling him when or how. It's very possible that he's tried to force a showdown."

"What are you going to do?"

"Difficult to say. Chevalier is still our agent and I don't want to put him in danger. I could arrest the German and William Sancenay, but that wouldn't get us to the core of the organization. If only I knew what Christopher had planned. In any case, if anyone asks you, say Bryce is in Paris. If they ask about me, tell them I'm a childhood friend."

"Are you planning to stay in Autun?" Claudine asked.

"What would I do there? I thought I would stay here with you." He paused. "You look as if you found that unsuitable."

"Why here?" Claudine asked to cover her confusion.

"Two reasons. One, if there is something afoot then you're going to need protection. Also, I have a feeling that if Christopher does resurface it will be here."

"What makes you think that?"

"Just intuition. I think that Chevalier is in love with you."

Claudine's fair skin flushed deeply. "That's very gallant of you, inspector, but I doubt if it's true." Her voice was unsteady.

Vidame studied her and a half smile played around his lips. "We'll see," he said finally. "We'll see."

Chapter 16

While Vidame went to get his car, which he had left outside the village, Claudine prepared his room and some dinner.

Claudine thought about the inspector's intuition. Her heart had raced at his words, but she told herself firmly that it just wasn't true, Christopher was not in love with her. He had played the role of kind and affectionate husband, but that was all. Except for that one slip at Amalfi, he had kept a friendly distance between them. And besides, he did not seem to be the type of man who fell in love easily.

Claudine was in the garden picking some lettuce for dinner when Mr. Dupin rang at the gate.

"Is your husband back?"

"He had to go to Paris unexpectedly."

Through the open window he could see into the dining room with the table laid for two.

"You aren't alone."

He was becoming annoyingly inquisitive, but Claudine had her explanation ready.

"An old friend is visiting. He's going to be staying for a few days."

"Won't your husband be upset?"

"This isn't the Middle Ages, Mr. Dupin."

Mr. Dupin was silent for a moment as if slightly offended.

"When Mr. Chevalier returns would you ask him to call at my house? I have something to show him that might interest him."

The old man took his leave courteously but somewhat stiffly, not able to hide his disapproval of Claudine's visitor.

Vidame was a pleasant guest. During dinner he conversed with ease and used so much tact in questioning her that it was a while before Claudine realized that she was being subjected to an interrogation.

"Inspector Vidame," she said finally, "would you do me a favor and not be so discreet? Please ask me directly what you want to know."

He smiled reassuringly. "I'm not trying to be discreet. The truth is that I don't know myself what I'm looking for. A phrase, a word, an allusion that might suggest what his intentions are."

"I really don't think that I can help you. All that I know is what Christopher deliberately chose to tell me. He doesn't usually let things slip out."

"I understand. We should get some sleep now. Tomorrow perhaps we'll be able to see things more clearly."

THE STORM THAT HAD THREATENED all day broke during the night. Claudine was awakened by the thunder and she could hear Vidame pacing in his room. He opened the drawers of the dresser, then those in the desk, then the wardrobe. Maybe he hoped Christopher had left behind some incriminating document. It all seemed very futile to Claudine.

The next morning as she passed Vidame his coffee she couldn't resist asking about his late night activity.

"Did your search reveal anything new?"

"Yes. Chevalier left behind all the papers in his brother's name that he'd been using. Surprised? Me, too. That means he's assumed his own identity again and I would love to know why."

Claudine, too, would have liked to know why, perhaps even more than the inspector. Had Christopher just grown tired of the whole charade and left? Or was he trying to double-cross the inspector? Claudine was afraid even to contemplate all the possibilities.

The telephone rang and Claudine hurried to answer it. An unfamiliar voice asked for Inspector Vidame. Claudine watched the inspector's face anxiously as he talked. When he hung up she looked at him inquiringly.

Vidame stared back grimly for a long moment before he could answer the question that was foremost on Claudine's mind.

"I didn't really expect this. It just goes to show that you never can tell." The inspector shook his head as if slightly bemused, then went on. "Yesterday evening Chevalier met with William Sancenay in Paris. He told William that he was in possession of information worth much more than the sum originally agreed on and that he had decided to sell it to the highest bidder."

The inspector paused again, seemingly still surprised by the information.

"It appears that Mr. Chevalier has decided to double-cross us."

Claudine looked at Vidame in anguish. Her heart crushed, she could feel the bitterness welling up inside her. How could Christopher have done this to them? And why? For money?

Claudine remembered the look in Christopher's eyes when he had left, the troubled expression of someone trying hard to say something, or to resist saying something. How could he have suddenly decided to double-cross her? She felt dizzy for a moment, as if she were perched on the edge of some great uncertainty. If she were to doubt Christopher now, everything would fall apart.

"I don't believe it," she said almost angrily to Vidame.

The inspector looked at her with a sort of appraisal.

"You don't believe he would do it, huh?"

"No, I don't. I'm not going to start doubting Christopher now. Your information must be wrong."

"Well, we'll soon find out. We have a microphone in William's apartment and their whole conversation was recorded. So pack your bags. We leave in ten minutes."

Without another word Claudine went upstairs and packed her suitcase. By the time she came down Vidame was at the wheel of his car. As they left Couhard, Claudine saw Mr. Dupin, with a look of scandalized horror on his face, watching them from the entrance to his garden.

When they reached Paris, Vidame dropped her off on the Champs-Elysées.

"I'll meet you at the coliseum in an hour," he told her, and then drove off.

The hour seemed to last for an eterntiy. When he

returned Claudine waited until she was in the car before asking any questions.

"What did you find out?"

"Quite a bit. For one thing, you're right. He's not trying to double-cross us. I found out that he's not trying to sell them information for the simple reason that he has none to sell. We have heard from a reliable source that they came across problems in their research several weeks ago in an area Chevalier couldn't help them with. So it turns out that he's trying to bluff them."

"Why is he doing that? Isn't it dangerous?"

"Dangerous? It's deadly! And, as for the reason that he's doing this, I can't be positive. Obviously if there's been a snag in the research, it could be many more months before we got any results. For one reason or another Chevalier didn't want to wait that long. My guess is that he became too concerned over your safety."

Claudine looked out the side window and bit her lip.

"I doubt if it's that," she replied. "He probably has just become tired of the game and wants to get it over with. Where are you taking me, anyway?"

"To Villeneuve-le-Roi, to a friend's house where you'll be safe. It's only about ten miles."

"Do you really think this is necessary?"

"Caution is always necessary, especially now."

His "friend" lived in a stone cottage surrounded by a lush suburban garden. She was a woman of about forty, who welcomed Claudine to the house without asking any questions. When Vidame asked for a tape recorder and played the tape in her presence Claudine realized that she was also working for Interpol.

They sat in the comfortable, old-fashioned living room and listened as the dialogue on the tape unfolded. Christopher was speaking authoritatively and William was unsuccessfully trying to reason with him. They were discussing a sum of money that Christopher was demanding, a sum so high that William was evidently flabbergasted.

"I have a taker at this price," Christopher affirmed, "but if the chief will match it, I'll give him preference."

"You're out of your mind!"

"No, I'm not. As long as I have this file, which is worth a fortune, I'm untouchable. But when I give up the information I'll need a guarantee, and the best guarantee I can have is to be in a position to be able to expose the chief."

"Did you think up this beautiful plan with Claudine? I thought it was suspicious when she suggested that she knew you weren't Bryce."

"Don't mix Claudine up in this! It has nothing to do with her."

The tape ended there.

"Did you understand what was going on?" Vidame asked.

"He wants the money to be handed over by the chief himself, supposedly in order to cover himself."

Vidame nodded. "Up to that point it's clear. But the problem is that he hasn't anything to sell, and it won't take long for them to find that out. In addition, he has no means of identifying the chief and anyone could pretend to be him."

"When you present it like that it sounds like a stupid plan." Claudine looked the inspector directly in the eye. "But Christopher isn't stupid."

That night, in a strange house, Claudine felt more lost than ever. She was drifting, with nothing to cling to. Who could she turn to? Vidame? His interest was purely professional. Could she turn to Christopher?

What had Christopher really meant to her, she wondered. He had been an imposter playing a role for reasons that had nothing to do with her. But still she missed him, missed him terribly.

"I NEED YOU," Vidame announced the following morning.

"Have you heard from Christopher?"

"We found him without too much difficulty because he stopped trying to hide from us. I'm going to have to make you responsible for finding out what his intentions are. He's staying at an inn near Rambouillet. I've rented a car, so you can drive over and see him."

"Do you think it's safe? What if the organization is watching him?"

"That's why I'm sending you. You believe he's your husband. What could be more natural than for you to go to see him?"

"Won't he want to know how I found him?"

"Tell him. And tell him about the recording. I want him to know how slender his margin for maneuver is. Even if we don't get him, the others will."

Since he obviously believed Christopher was in danger, Claudine wondered why he didn't intervene.

"Couldn't you arrest him or something?"

"For what? Fraud? We aren't in a very good position to do that! No, if you can't convince him that what he's doing is stupid then all we can do is watch and wait."

The inn where Christopher was hiding had the romantic charm of a lovers' hideaway. It was small and rustic, set in the middle of a park with two rows of plane trees around the edge, a river and a few tables. At one of the tables Christopher was sitting reading, so absorbed that Claudine had time to approach him at her leisure. Looking at him Claudine tried to match him with all that she had so recently learned about him. But all she could see was the kind husband that she had learned to love so dearly over the past few months, the man with whom she had shared a happiness she had never known before.

As she approached he raised his head and for the space of a second joy flashed into his eyes. But he was instantly in control of himself again.

"This is a visit I hadn't hoped for," he said warmly as he stood up.

"Are you annoyed?"

"I should have known you would come. Did Vidame send you?"

"Yes. He seems to have taken me into his protection."

"On the condition that you persuade me to confess?"

"Unconditionally. As far as he's concerned the demands you made on the organization are naive."

"How does he know what I demanded?"

Claudine told him about the microphone and he started to laugh.

"The department is improving. What exactly is Vidame angry about? I've rushed his program but if I succeed he'll be the last to complain."

"If you succeed. He thinks that they'll just send you one of the minions in the organization who will pretend to be the boss and you'll have achieved nothing."

"I wouldn't have done this if I couldn't identify the boss. I have an idea who he is and I won't give my file over to anyone else but him."

"Vidame claims you have no file."

"Then he certainly underestimates me. I've concocted one that is convincing enough. All I had to do was present a few probabilities as facts. Durand helped. He's pressed for time, too. If the members of the organization aren't arrested soon, he'll kill himself."

"And you? Are you sure you know the risks you are taking?"

"I've known them for a long time, and I'm sure I know what I'm doing."

His confidence didn't reassure Claudine. On the contrary, it made her worry even more. Still, she couldn't bring herself to ask him the question that was the most important to her: why was he doing this?

Christopher invited her to stay for lunch and all through the meal Claudine tried unsuccessfully to get him to give up his dangerous plan. When she finally ran out of arguments she ended up begging.

"Suppose I asked you to give up for my sake?"

He smiled. "Thank you for pretending to care. But it's too late to go back now. I wish Vidame hadn't mixed you up in this mess."

"I was already in it."

"No you weren't. It hasn't anything to do with you now. The organization thinks I'm Durand and as far as they are concerned there's no longer any connection between the two of us."

"What are you going to do now?"

"Wait. It won't be much longer."

Chapter 17

"Does he think they won't retaliate?" Vidame exploded. "I was counting on you to succeed. However, since you didn't, you'd better stay here where you'll be safe."

He gave Claudine his number and told her that if anything at all came up she was to call him.

For forty-eight hours Claudine stayed in Villeneuve, living the life of a recluse. Nothing new happened. Things seemed to be moving much more slowly than she had expected. Claudine decided that if she was going to be away any longer she at least ought to call old Mr. Dupin and tell him, so that he could keep an eye on the house.

"At last!" Dupin cried as soon as he heard her voice. "You must come right away! Something terrible has come up!"

"What? What's wrong?"

"It's terrible! It's about your husband, but I can't tell you over the phone. Just come home quickly!"

The old man sounded so beside himself with distress that the only way Claudine could calm him down was to assure him that she would be there right away.

As the hostess of the house she was staying at was out, Claudine left her a note explaining her sudden departure. Then she rented a car at the nearest garage and drove as fast as the law would allow. The old man's confused words had worried her. What if the organization had done something to Christopher just as they had to Bryce? Trying not to think about it Claudine drove on. At midday she stopped in a restaurant for coffee and telephoned Vidame.

"You're a very foolhardy young lady. This could just be some sort of a trap. Did he say anything specific?"

"No, but he sounded extremely upset. Anyway, the old man is too harmless to be part of any kind of trap."

"Even so, stay where you are, and I'll go to Couhard instead."

"That's out of the question!"

He started to protest, but Claudine had hung up.

When Claudine got to Mr. Dupin's house, the old man was waiting out in front for her and excitedly signaled her to stop.

"What's happened?" Claudine demanded immediately. "Where's my husband?"

"He's not here. Come in and let me explain."

Claudine followed him into the library.

"Please tell me what happened. Is Bryce in the hospital?"

"Try to stay calm. You are going to need a lot of courage for what I have to tell you. Your husband. . . oh. . .how difficult this is!"

His awkwardness was driving her crazy. Expecting the worst, Claudine no longer had the courage to ask any questions.

"Ever since yesterday," he said, "I've been trying to find the words to make this terrible news easier. There are none. Your husband is dead."

Claudine stared at the old man in disbelief. If Christopher had been killed surely Vidame would have told her when she called him. Even if Christopher had dropped back out of sight the inspector would have said something. Claudine refused to believe the old man's words.

"That's impossible," she said flatly.

"I'm afraid there is more to this. I have some information that is unfortunately indisputable. You have been the victim of a monstrous fraud. The man you have been living with is an impostor. Your husband died in August of last year."

Claudine was overcome with relief when she realized what Dupin was talking about. She feigned incredulity.

"Surely you don't really mean this, Mr. Dupin. I know my husband and no one could take his place without me realizing it. The idea is absolutely ridiculous. Perhaps it was the operation he had that gave you this idea."

"At first. But I always had doubts about his identity, and as I was interested in you I decided to conduct a few inquiries. I found out that the surgeon who operated on your husband was arrested recently. And since then your husband has admitted it himself."

Claudine was beginning to get suspicious. She knew that Christopher would never have admitted such a thing to the old man.

"He told you he wasn't my husband? That's ridiculous! He must have been playing a joke on you."

"It wasn't to me that he admitted it, it was to William Sancenay. You see, it's a matter of industrial espionage."

Mr. Dupin then went on to tell Claudine the whole story about the substitution. The only difference between his story and Christopher's story was that the old man didn't know about the double switch and thought that Christopher was the chemist, Durand.

"And William told you all of this?" Claudine asked when he was through.

"Yes, we discussed the matter when he was here visiting you."

Claudine knew that he was lying. William would not have exposed himself in such a way. The only way that Mr. Dupin could have this information was if the charming old man, lover of fine houses and amateur historian, was a part of the organization.

Claudine stared at what she used to think was a harmless old man and wondered what she should do. She decided that the safest thing would be to continue playing her role, pretending that she knew nothing of what was going on.

"The only way I could believe any of this is if I heard it from Bryce himself."

"He'll confirm it. Sancenay is bringing him here tomorrow morning and we'll make him tell you everything. In the meantime, let me offer you a room for the night. You'll be safer here than alone in your own house."

Vidame was right, it was a trap! Claudine's only chance lay in forcing Dupin to play his hand. He hadn't yet exposed himself as a member of the organization. If she played her own role well enough, he would be forced either to let her go or to admit his involvement.

"It's kind of you to offer," Claudine said, "but I think I'd rather go home."

"When you're so upset? Don't even consider it."

She argued the matter at length but with no success. He had a good reply to every argument she put forward. When Claudine started for the door he blocked her way and, smiling, locked the door.

"Are you making me a prisoner?"

"For your own good, dear lady, for your own good!"

His manner was so natural that he could very easily have passed as a sincere and concerned neighbor. Claudine gave up.

"Very well, I agree to stay, but I ought to get my suitcase from the car."

"I'll look after that. Let me show you your room so that you'll have time to rest before dinner. You've been through a very tiring ordeal."

Claudine had no other choice but to go along with the charade. She couldn't insist on leaving without giving away how much she knew. And that would be a deadly mistake.

Claudine sat in her room and tried to think of what she should do. She wasn't sure what Dupin hoped to gain by holding her prisoner but she didn't plan to wait around to find out. She would sneak out during the night. If the gates were locked she would find a ladder and climb over the wall. She would be giving herself away, but once she was out of the organization's clutches that wouldn't matter.

That evening at dinner, for the first time since she

had met him, Dupin did not discuss local history. He had prepared a cold meal, which he served himself, all the while continuing to try to persuade her that she had been a widow for several months. With equal obstinacy Claudine feigned complete disbelief, although she knew the truth far better than he did. Immediately after dinner she excused herself to go to bed.

"Make yourself quite at home," he said, "and sleep well. You are in no danger here. I electrified the walls and the gates in order to discourage unwelcome visitors. At the least movement, the burglar alarm will sound, and I'm armed."

Claudine did not miss the underlying threat in his words. If she tried to escape she'd be shot.

In bed that night, Claudine went over the situation in her mind. She was convinced that her life was in immediate danger. As long as she continued to play her role and act as if she believed that Dupin was just an overprotective neighbor, the organization would have no reason to fear her. If they were trying to use her as a hostage to bargain for the information that Christopher said he possessed, Claudine didn't think it would work. And besides, Christopher didn't really have any information to sell. Her only aid from the outside would be Vidame. He knew where she was going and had suspected a trap. Maybe he would get worried enough to come and investigate. Or maybe not.

Claudine was unable to sleep all night. At dawn the song of the thrush replaced the rustling of the insects, the sky grew pale, and the sunlight crept into the room. Claudine was convinced that Christopher would not show up as Mr. Dupin expected and that the old man would then let her go, thinking that he had nothing to lose by doing so and nothing to gain by keeping her.

When the doorbell rang at eight o'clock, Claudine was already dressed. She went downstairs and found Dupin in the hallway with William. As she had suspected, William had arrived alone.

"Already up?" asked Dupin. "I hope you didn't sleep badly?"

Claudine ignored his remark and addressed William.

"William, would you kindly tell Mr. Dupin that the crazy story you told him before was all a joke."

"I'm afraid it's not a joke, Claudine. The real name of the man you call Bryce is Durand. He told me everything. I don't understand why you don't believe it since you were the first to put the idea into my head."

"But I proved that he *is* Bryce."

"You imagined it, because that's the way you wanted it to be. He gave me too much information for there to be any doubt. Bryce was selling information to foreign agents. He drowned in a lake last summer and the agents hit on the idea of substituting Durand, who is a chemist, in his place. Leroux took care of altering his face. Everyone was taken in, myself included."

"You told me that Bryce was coming so that I could talk to him."

"He refused," William said. "Which is further proof that he isn't your husband. Bryce would have come immediately if he knew you were here and . . . ." He stopped himself, suddenly aware of his mistake.

"And what?"

"And you thought he was dead," Dupin replied, coming to William's aid. "If this story, as you call it, wasn't true, he would certainly have been in a hurry to let you know."

"Believe me," insisted William, "this man doesn't care about what happens to you."

"I think Bryce wanted to pay me back for being suspicious and that this is just a bad joke he's playing," Claudine said, trying to maintain her role. "Maybe the best thing would be for me to go home. It was very kind of you to take me in, Mr. Dupin, but I don't want to abuse your hospitality."

The old man raised his hands to the ceiling, looking distressed.

"I can't let you leave like this. That man is dangerous and who knows what he might be capable of now, if you were ever alone with him."

"You aren't going to force me to stay, are you?"

"Only if necessary, my dear lady."

Dupin was smiling, but he was also blocking the door.

"How long do you intend to keep me here?"

"Just until your so-called husband comes to find you."

"And if he doesn't come?"

From the top of the stairs a voice replied, "And why wouldn't I come?"

Speechless, Claudine watched Christopher casually walk down the stairs.

"How did you get in?" Dupin's smile had vanished.

"Over the wall, across the garden and through a window. Your alarm system is badly designed. If I were you I would complain to the company that designed it. It's easily disconnected."

Recovering from his surprise, Dupin forced a smile.

"Why did you go to so much trouble? You were invited."

"I prefer to take the initiative," Christopher replied smoothly. "It's a bad habit I have."

Claudine realized the risks that Christopher was taking and she was scared.

"Bryce! Why did you come?"

"To take you home, my dear. If it is all the same to you, Mr. Dupin, I would prefer leaving through the door. My wife is not trained for windows."

"Your wife!" William cried. "Surely you aren't going to try to continue this absurd masquerade! You aren't Bryce. Bryce is dead."

Christopher looked genuinely astonished.

"You, too! First Claudine and now you, a friend for twenty years. You suspect me, too?"

"You deny it? You dare deny it?" William was beside himself with rage.

Dupin calmed him with a gesture.

"Don't let's get angry over this. We know you took Bryce's place, Durand, so you can stop your little game now."

"I took Bryce's place where? What are you talking about?"

Dupin's attitude and his voice suddenly changed.

"All right, Durand, we can stop this little game. I am not just an inquisitive old man, I happen to be your boss. You don't need to pretend in front of me. I have no more time to waste on this. You have something to sell and you know my conditions."

"First, let Claudine go."

"She will leave when I have the papers."

Christopher had moved forward so that now he stood between Dupin and Claudine.

"So? Claudine's freedom against my file? What makes you think I'll accept the deal? She isn't important to me."

"If that were true you wouldn't have come. My offer is final."

Claudine thought she heard footsteps on the second floor but no one paid any attention. Christopher raised his voice slightly.

"Not only do I not have a file, but I'm not even a chemist."

"What do you hope to gain from this, Durand?"

"I am not Durand. Your little substitution game can be played more than once."

This time the footsteps were quite clear. Claudine turned and saw Vidame on the stairs. Suddenly Christopher threw her to the ground and there was the sound of gunfire.

Her head hit the ground with a crack and everything went black.

Chapter 18

Slowly Claudine regained consciousness. With a great effort she opened her eyes. The first thing that she saw was the open window and the sky turning pink with dusk. The evening breeze carried the sounds of birds and of the cathedral bells sounding for evening Mass.

She realized that she was back in her room at Couhard. She tried to remember what had happened, but all she could recall was the terror and the deafening noise of gunshots.

Footsteps approached along the hall. The door opened and Inspector Vidame came in.

"You're back with us, are you?" he said jovially

"Where's Christopher?"

"Christopher's in the hospital. He got a bullet in his arm. Nothing serious. They'll have him fixed up in no time."

"What happened?"

"Can't remember, huh? Well, I guess you did have quite a fall." Vidame laughed as if he found it funny.

"Which is rather lucky, really. Not that you fell, of course, but that Chevalier has such excellent reflexes. It seems that our honorable Mr. Dupin completely lost his head and started shooting like a madman. Which gave us all the more reason to arrest him." Vidame continued to chuckle, as if he found the whole affair supremely amusing.

"How is it you were there?" Claudine asked, still not clear on all that had happened.

"Chevalier called me as soon as William gave him the organization's ultimatum."

"What ultimatum?"

"Sancenay told him you were being held hostage and would be released only when he handed over his file. Christopher refused, of course. But you should have heard him when he called me!" Vidame shook his head. "Of course I suppose I deserved being called a few names. After all, he was the one doing all the work, and all I had to do was keep an eye on you and then I let you get caught in a trap like that. Anyway, after yelling at me for a while, he calmed down enough for me to tell him that I knew where you were, or at least where you had been headed.

"It seems that Chevalier had suspected Dupin for some time. He found his role as the old eccentric too good to be true. So we drove to Couhard together and climbed the wall during the night after Chevalier had disconnected the alarm. We hid in the attic until Sancenay arrived. We didn't want you to be a victim when we intervened so Chevalier went downstairs alone at first. You know the rest."

"Why did Dupin try to shoot Christopher?"

"He tried to shoot you. If Chevalier hadn't intervened you would probably have been killed. I sup-

pose he intended to shoot you both and claim that
he had hit you while aiming for Durand. The man
is a gifted liar. He is still telling us everything
except the truth but we have enough charges
against him to put him out of circulation for a few
years."

"A few years! For murder?" Claudine was aghast.

"What murder? He swears Bryce's death was accidental, which is what Durand and Sancenay say, as
well. I personally believe that it wasn't accidental,
but I can't prove anything. We'll have to be satisfied
with pressing other charges that we know we can
make stick. Incidentally, the official story at the trial
will mention only the first substitution of Durand's
taking your husband's place. When you're ques-
tioned you're to say that after he took Bryce's place,
Durand regretted it and got in touch with the police.
He'll get away with a minimum sentence. You should
say that you knew about it all along and agreed to
help us."

"But what about Christopher?"

"He doesn't want anything more to do with it. He
says that he's planning to leave as soon as his arm is
patched up and that he doesn't want to stick around
for the trial."

"He's leaving?" Claudine felt her heart wrench inside of her.

Vidame looked at her seriously. "Yes. Chevalier
isn't the type to stay in one place too long. It's a
shame, too. A guy like that could really be an asset if
only I could talk him into joining Interpol."

Claudine wasn't listening. She was staring out the
window at the falling night, trying very hard to hold
back her tears.

THE NEXT MORNING Claudine's friend Sophie drove down from Paris to stay with her at Couhard for a week. Claudine had called her and told her everything that had happened and her friend had insisted on coming down to visit. Claudine was extremely thankful. She did not want to be alone.

Sophie fixed some lunch while Claudine told her all the details of what had happened.

"Well, thank goodness it's over," Sophie said sympathetically.

"Yes, thank goodness," Claudine agreed, but her voice sounded so sad that Sophie looked at her closely, wondering if she meant it.

Just then there was a knock on the door, and Sophie answered it. It was Christopher, his arm in a sling and a small traveling suitcase in his good hand.

"Well, I'm on my way," he said lightly, avoiding Claudine's eyes. "Just thought I'd drop by to say so long."

Claudine looked at him and the tears that had been threatening all morning suddenly vanished. Fury rose in their place. "How nice of you to think of me," she retorted sarcastically.

Christopher blinked and took a step backward. "Well, yes, and I wanted to thank you for . . . for . . . ." His voice trailed off.

"Yes? For what? What is it you want to thank me for? For my good cooking? For worrying myself sick over you? What is it?"

Christopher was obviously embarrassed. "I didn't mean it to happen this way, Claudine. I know how you must feel, but—"

"But what? But you just can't give up your life of gay adventure? Well, what are you waiting for then?

You don't expect me to pack you a lunch, do you? If you're going to go, go. Don't worry about me. I can get along just fine without you."

Christopher stared at her, quite stunned, struggling for a moment to say something. Then, giving up, he turned and slammed out of the house.

Sophie, surprised by the whole scene, comforted Claudine, who had broken down crying as soon as Christopher had gone. She insisted that Claudine pack up her things immediately and come back with her to Paris. Claudine could stay with Sophie in her apartment and they would start another boutique.

Claudine, not knowing what else to do, agreed with her friend's plans. She certainly didn't want to stay in Couhard after all that had happened there, and she didn't really have anywhere else to go.

They spent the day organizing and packing. Claudine didn't talk much. Her mind was still numb from all that had happened. Everything had moved so fast that she hadn't had time to think about what was going to happen when it was all over. Now she thought about the real Bryce and felt pangs of remorse, realizing that much of his bad humor must have stemmed from the pressure of trying to act as a sort of double agent. True, he had brought it all on himself, but she couldn't help feeling sorry nonetheless.

And then there was Christopher, the man she had learned to love while he was disguised as Bryce, but had not been able to stop loving even after she had learned the truth. What had she really expected from him? Everything she knew about him pointed to his being an adventurer. If she had thought about it she would have known that he couldn't be tied down. But she had never thought about it, and in the back of her mind she had always believed that he would still be there when it was all over. But he was gone now, and the look in his eye that she had thought was affection must have been pity. She was just going to have to learn to live without him. Although that might take a very long time.

AFTER PACKING, Claudine and Sophie decided to go out to dinner. They got dressed up and went out to the Old Windmill. Claudine wanted to have a good time and enjoy all the fancy food and wine, but her heart just wasn't in it. She was silent throughout most of the meal and Sophie, sympathetic and understanding, did not press her.

It was dark by the time they returned home. When Claudine went to open the door she noticed that there was a light on, but she assumed that they had left it on by mistake. She had taken three or four steps into the house before she saw him.

He was standing in the living room, a glass in his hand. The single light picked up the gold highlights in his dark hair. His eyes were in shadow.

"Christopher!" Claudine was dumbfounded.

Without a word, Christopher set the glass down on the table. Sophie, who had followed Claudine in, glanced questioningly from Claudine to Christopher and back again.

"I think I'll be off to bed now," Sophie announced, moving toward the stairs. But the other two didn't seem to hear her.

Slowly and purposefully Christopher began walking toward Claudine, who hesitantly backed up.

"How did you get in?" she asked nervously, remembering even as she said it that he still had a key.

Christopher didn't say anything as he closed the distance between them. She had now run out of room and stood with her back against the door. Her pulse was racing as she looked up into the handsome face that had become so dear and familiar to her.

"Christopher, what is it?" she asked, while searching his dark eyes, not daring to believe the answer she found there. Her knees grew weak and her stomach fluttered as he gazed down at her.

"What's wrong? Did you forget something?" she faltered, her voice trembling in spite of her efforts to control it.

"Yes," Christopher said, lifting her chin gently with his good hand. "I forgot the most important thing of all."

As he bent to kiss her she heard him whisper, "I forgot my wife."

What readers say about Mystique Books

"Mystique Books are so exciting
and fast-moving that it really *is*
hard to put them down."
L.R. and M.R.* Pennsburg, Pennsylvania

"Mystique Books let you relax and
enjoy your imagination."
W.E.D., West Allis, Wisconsin

"Mystique Books are exciting, romantic,
interesting and mysterious. I
can hardly put them down."
E.R., Waterford, Wisconsin

*Names available on request.

MYSTIQUE BOOKS

Experience the warmth of love... and the threat of danger!

MYSTIQUE BOOKS are a breathless blend of romance and suspense, passion and mystery. Let them take you on journeys to exotic lands—the sunny Caribbean, the enchantment of Paris, the sinister streets of Istanbul.

MYSTIQUE BOOKS

An unforgettable reading experience.
Now... many previously published titles are once again available.
Choose from this great selection!

Don't miss any of these thrilling novels of love and adventure!

Choose from this list of exciting
MYSTIQUE BOOKS